THE HIDDEN HORSE

THE HIDDEN HORSE

Josephine Pullein-Thompson

Allen Junior Fiction

THE HIDDEN HORSE *was first published as*
ALL CHANGE *by Ernest Benn Ltd in 1961.*
Armada Edition 1963
Fontana retitled edition 1982
Revised Allen Junior Fiction edition 1989
Text © Josephine Pullein-Thompson
Illustrations © J A Allen 1989

to **ALEXANDER**

British Library Cataloguing in Publication Data
Pullein-Thompson, Josephine
The hidden horse.
I. Title
823'.914 [J]
ISBN 0 85131 490 2

Printed in Malta by Interprint Limited

ONE

When I came home for the Christmas holidays I found the inhabitants of Nutsford Farmhouse unusually gloomy. The human inhabitants that is; Storm, our black Labrador, was her usual bouncing, grinning self.

We had known all summer that old Lord Charnworth's death would mean changes and that death duties would force his son to sell the Charnworth Estate, but now the changes had come about and I gathered that the new owner, a Mr. Daniel Smithson, was far from perfect.

I had better explain that my father, John Conway, had been agent to old Lord Charnworth for almost eight years and had looked after the farms, woods and cottages on the Charnworth Estate until they began to seem like his own. We, the five Conway children, all loved Charnworth: the big house, the yellow stone village, the brook running through the park to join the small winding river Spay, and the great downs of North Barset which sheltered us to the east and west. Naturally we were very concerned by the character of the new owner; even our house belonged to him.

My first supper at home was deadly. Andrew and

Rory were on their way to bed; we don't stay up to supper in our family until we are twelve – Andrew still has a year to go and poor Rory nearly four – and Dad said he would seize the opportunity to "talk to you older ones seriously". My father is a biggish man with dark hair and sad brown eyes; Cathy and Andrew are the most like him though Cathy has a gayer nature and Andrew's eyes are blue. The rest of us, Penny, Rory and I, are supposed to be like our Scottish grandfather; we have sandy hair and light blue eyes and we're wiry instead of being well-built like Dad and Andrew or possessing neat figures like Mum and Cathy. It's a pity that Penny doesn't look more like our mother because, though not a raving beauty or madly exotic or anything like that, Mum manages to look much better than most people's mothers and really rather stands out when you see them in the mass at school speech days or sports.

Dad looked at us sorrowfully and sighed, "Now look, Douglas," he said, "we're going through a very difficult time here at the moment. I don't know how I'm going to get on with Mr. Smithson and it's possible that I may have to change my job, but we all love Charnworth so much that it would be a terrible wrench to leave and if I *can* work with him I will. Now the point is that we've got into the habit of treating the place rather as though it belonged to us. Old Lord Charnworth didn't mind, in fact he often told me how much he liked to see you all enjoying yourselves. I think in a way he looked upon you as grandchildren, but Smithson isn't going to feel like that; we've got to realise that we're starting all over again from scratch and we can't expect any of the privileges we've enjoyed in the past."

"No races in the park," I said, "no picnics in the

castle ruins or short cuts through the stableyard or begging windfall peaches from old Mr. White."

"No, definitely not." Dad looked at me gravely. "You're the eldest, Douglas, and you must try to be responsible."

Everyone thinks I'm irresponsible and I've decided that it's the fault of my face. I haven't got a very dignified face. It's a bit freckled and my nose isn't big enough; I've noticed that people with hooked noses and Roman noses, and even large red fleshy noses are never accused of irresponsibility. And then my mouth is too big and instead of smiling sadly like Dad I always go and give a great grin; Cathy says it's from ear to ear, but that is an exaggeration. And then I don't usually feel dismal so it's very difficult to go about in a sad and sober manner, but as for being irresponsible I don't think it's true. I've kept Rory away from ponds and rivers and cars for eight years now and at school I'm no worse than most people. Dad said, "You remember that gate you smashed up when you tried to jump it last Easter? Lord Charnworth didn't mind, I know, but I've a strong feeling that Mr. Smithson would. You're to keep strictly to the lanes and bridlepaths and if not sure about any ride don't go it until you've asked me. Don't jump *any* of his fences, not even low ones; just try to remember that a lot may depend upon your behaviour these holidays."

"O.K.," I said. "We'll be models of tact."

Dad looked at me and sighed so I suppose he thought I was being flippant, but I didn't feel flippant; the thought of leaving Nutsford made me feel quite sick, but I couldn't see any point in going round with a long face until it actually happened.

Mum said, "Look, don't tell Andrew and Rory that

we might have to move, they're a bit young to be worried with things like that and Rory will only have nightmares. "

We said we wouldn't and then I asked, "What does he look like? Smithson, I mean."

It turned out that no one but Dad had met him yet though Mum had seen both him and Mrs. Smithson in the distance and the whole family had been scouring the gossip and financial columns of the newspapers in which they were sometimes mentioned; Andrew had cut out the best one for his scrapbook; in it Mr. Smithson was described as a "financial wizard" and Mrs. Smithson as wearing "fabulous furs".

Dad said, "He's in his fifties; he has grey hair and spectacles. He's just about as tall as I am and a bit on the fat side. He's supposed to be a billionaire."

He sighed. "I'm spoilt," he said. "I don't suppose if I live to be a hundred I'll ever find another employer like Lord Charnworth."

Mum sighed too as she got up to clear the table. "And I do love this house," she said. "Why don't we save, John, instead of spending our money? We might have had enough to buy a farm of our own."

"Hardly," answered Dad. "You haven't Mr. Smithson's ability to calculate, Fi (her name is Fiona); it would take more than twelve years on a land-agent's salary to save enough for a farm."

Cathy, Penny and I helped to clear away and wash up and then we wandered along the kitchen passage and down the stone steps to our room, which is the oldest part of the farmhouse and was once a kitchen. It is long and narrow with a low ceiling and the beams are full of hooks on which sides of bacon and strings of onions used to hang. There is an enormous fireplace and a lot of shelves, which are useful for books and displays of Red Indians, farm animals or Dinky cars, and several large, dark cupboards which make tidying up easy as you just chuck everything in and force the door shut.

We lit the oil heater and crouched round it while the girls told me how dismal things were and what ages it took to walk to the field at the Firs which Dad had rented for the ponies, since Mr. Smithson could hardly be expected to let us use Long Meadow as we had in Lord Charnworth's time.

Soon, what with feeling dismal and the fact that the old kitchen hadn't been used enough lately to get warmed up, we began to freeze and we decided to go up to the girls' bedroom which has a really efficient electric fire. We hadn't been there long when Andrew and Rory appeared; they were wearing pyjamas, tartan rugs and Indian headdresses.

"Go back to bed," we said sternly.

"Won't," answered Rory. "Go to the devil." And Andrew, always more reasonable, explained, "Rory can't sleep and he wakes me up every two minutes by asking if I'm awake and now you're all up here talking it's hopeless."

"Let them stay for a bit," suggested Cathy and rather grudgingly we made room for them by the fire.

Then we couldn't talk about the awful possibility of having to leave Nutsford any more so we just sat and grumbled about Mr. Smithson.

"All the rides are ruined," complained Penny, "and there's nothing to jump, not even the fallen-down trees in the park."

"They're not all ruined," remonstrated Cathy.

"There's still the downs and the tracks to the river and the bridlepath on Forest Hill."

"Yes, I know, but you can't make a decent round any more," grumbled Penny, "and I hate coming back the same way as I went out. I'd like to put a curse on Mr. Smithson; he's ruining everything."

"You could make a waxen image and stick pins into it," suggested Andrew dreamily.

"That wouldn't make him go away," said Penny. "He'd just think he had rheumatism and call in a Harley Street specialist."

"He might think the climate of Charnworth had given him the rheumatism," I suggested, "and that would send him flying back to Mayfair or wherever he hangs out."

"Of course *he* hasn't actually said that we're not to ride through the park," Cathy pointed out. "It's just that Dad doesn't feel like asking for permission yet."

"I wish he'd hurry up and ask about Long Meadow," said Penny. "It wastes ages every single day walking up to the Firs and, anyway, it'll seem awfully silly if we don't ride in the park for months and then when Dad asks him he says it's all right."

"But you've got to be tactful at first," I told her. "Billionaires need very careful handling."

"And Dad doesn't like asking favours," said Cathy.

"And I don't blame him," I added, "it's beastly, especially from people you don't like."

We were silent for a little and then I said, "If only we could do something for Mr. Smithson; something that filled him with eternal gratitude, then he'd say, with a choke in his voice, 'Conway, if there's anything I can do for those children of yours any time just let me know.'

Surely *then* Dad would mention Long Meadow."

"I bet he wouldn't," Penny was determined to be pessimistic, "he'd say, 'That's quite all right, Mr. Smithson, it's a pleasure; please don't mention it,' and we'd have to go on walking all the way to the Firs. Besides, what can you do for billionaires? He can pay people vast sums to do anything he wants done."

"We could save his life," suggested Andrew. "We could plunge fully dressed into the lake when he was drowning."

"Even if he was idiotic enough to fall into the lake, he jolly well ought to be able to swim," objected Penny.

"I bet he can't," said Rory, who can't swim himself.

"The house might catch fire," suggested Cathy, "or thieves might steal Mrs. Smithson's fabulous furs, but I don't see how we're going to get near enough to see what's going on if we're not allowed in the park."

"The path from South Lodge to the church," said Penny, "that's a right of way, surely?"

"It might not be a bridlepath," I said, "but there's a hunting gate at either end so probably it is. Yes, that gets us quite near to the house and practically on the brink of the lake. We could do a sort of daily patrol."

"I wish we could meet him," said Andrew, "after all, he might *like* us; people do sometimes. At least old Lord Charnworth seemed to, even though he couldn't remember our names and always called Douglas David."

"He liked tough types," I pointed out, "he thought we were daring, but I shouldn't think we were Mr. Smithson's type. He probably likes studious-looking boys who are mad about maths, and lady-like girls, not hooligans with matted hair like Penny."

At this point Penny attacked me and as we rolled giggling on the floor the others beat us with pillows. Soon Mum's voice from downstairs inquired what was going on and announced that it was time we were all in bed. Andrew and Rory scuttled off guiltily and the rest of us began to argue about who needed baths.

TWO

The first day of the holidays was as wet and windy as most of the other days in December had been. But, despite the sound of rain lashing against the windows and the wind whistling theatrically round the house, my sisters announced at breakfast that they had fetched home and fed the ponies and that it was my turn to ride Merlin, as they had had him all the term, but Cathy would squeeze herself on Jessica, Penny would borrow Harlequin and they would accompany me.

Living in the depths of the country and eight miles from Spayborne, the nearest town, riding has always been one of our main occupations, but, since we only possessed two ponies between five of us an elaborate system of turns had to be worked out. Our ponies, Merlin, a strawberry roan of barely fourteen hands, and Jessica, a sturdy bay of 12.3 with black points and a huge white blaze, are both elderly and were passed on to us by other families in the neighbourhood. In the summer, before Lord Charnworth died, our parents had talked of buying a small horse for me to ride in the holidays and Cathy in term, but now, with this grim feeling of impending change in the air, the subject of a third mount was dropped.

When the rain slackened slightly we began to collect macintoshes; mine had become hopelessly small, once on it acted as a strait-jacket and held my arms tightly to my sides. Penny bagged it quickly, though a year younger than Cathy she is very nearly the same size so there is always competition for my outgrown clothes. Andrew, bewailing the fact that Penny's cast-offs were always beltless and buttonless, booked her mac and I searched under the stairs until I found an army surplus garment of Dad's which hung on me like a monk's robe, but looked waterproof. Owing to Mum's contention that falling on our heads might make us more idiotic than we are already, we are always kept well supplied with riding hats and mine still fitted. I felt rather reluctant when the moment came to leave Andrew and Rory playing comfortably in the old kitchen with Andrew's electric train – a birthday present from a rich godfather. However, we made a bold dash from the back door to the stable and then Penny departed on a bicycle for the Old Rectory while Cathy and I groomed.

Nutsford Farmhouse is really in two halves. There is the very old bit, low, beamed, with lopsided windows and crooked walls in which are the old kitchen, various boot holes and a sort of cloakroom downstairs, and two rather attic-like bedrooms, allotted to us boys, upstairs. The rest of the house is Jacobean and rather handsome with mullioned windows and an oak front door. It is all built of the local yellowish-grey stone and has a stone-tiled roof. It is a nice house, not at all grand, and in the summer there is a terrifically sweet smell from the roses which climb all over it. The Lord Charnworth before last took Nutsford's land away and joined it up with the

Home Farm land, just keeping the house for his agent, and not using the farm buildings which gradually had fallen down or been cleared away until now when there was nothing left but the long stone stable, partly turned into a garage and a great stone barn, standing at the top of Long Meadow, which is used for storing hay. The stable isn't grand either. There is a loose box at either end and two stalls in between and the ponies look out on the passageway of the stable, which may be dull sometimes, but is nice on wet days.

My heart sank rather when I saw Merlin; he seemed to have shrunk since the summer holidays and, though I am not particularly tall for my age, which is fifteen – just – I could see that my feet were going to be dangling round his knees. He made out he was pleased to see me and, as I attempted to groom off the wet mud, he amused himself by searching for the pockets in Dad's army surplus garment. As one would imagine from his name he is a wise-looking pony with a long lean head, but the people who had him before us say that he had the wise expression years ago when he was young and frivolous and that it comes from the two saltcellar-like hollows above his eyes, the result, they say, of having an old mother.

"Jess is in a furious temper," Cathy called to me from the other loose box, "she says it's ridiculous to go out in this weather and we shall all catch our deaths of cold."

"Tell her not to be such an old fuss-pot," I answered. Jess is twenty. We are the fourth family she has taught to ride; she thinks us very young and foolish and treats us with great contempt and for some reason she is supposed to talk like old Mrs. Guppy at the West Lodge who was once nurse to old Lord Charnworth's children.

We mounted in the narrow cobbled yard and set off up our lane, past the back drive to Charnworth House, and on the road we turned right for the village.

As we reached the Old Rectory Penny led Harlequin out. "He's filthy," she said indignantly, "and it won't come off."

Harlequin certainly didn't look very elegant; his fat piebald body was a uniform mud colour, his mane, unhogged since the beginning of the summer holidays, stood up in a bristling brush and, as Penny mounted he rolled his small eyes and made a dash for the grass verge. Penny hauled him away.

"The rain'll clean him up," I said. "Are we going to patrol the park first?"

"Yes, let's," answered Cathy, "I do want to see them; it's awfully hard to work up a hate against people you've never seen."

I asked, "Why try? It won't do any good. I mean, either Dad gets on with Mr. S. or else he doesn't; there's no point in trying to work up a feud."

"Don't you mind beastly London people coming to live at Charnworth?" asked Penny indignantly as we rode past Home Farm. "Everybody in the village is furious."

"No, I don't see that London people have got to be beastly," I answered, "and anyway someone had to buy the place. Would you rather it was turned into a school, because then the farms would have been sold off separately and Dad would have been out of a job?"

"I'd rather the Honourable Bob had been able to keep it up and everything had gone on just as before," said Penny. The Hon Bob, as he has always been called locally, is Lord Charnworth's eldest son and now, of course, Lord Charnworth.

We rode into the village. About sixteen stone cottages, one of them the post office, clustered about the main or south gates of Charnworth and, close to the lodge, a hunting-gate opened into a narrow wood, known as Home Farm Spinney, through which ran the path to the church. Penny insisted on opening the gate and she and Harlequin had a long and boring battle while Merlin and Jess stood in the rain seething at such equine incompetence. They are both champion gate-openers and use their chests and noses to such purpose that the rider is hardly necessary. At first the path runs parallel to the south drive with its avenue of beech trees, but when you enter the park it turns right-handed towards the church and the back drive. Usually we set off at a gallop the moment we are in the park, for it seems a waste of time to walk or trot on such a tempting stretch of springy turf, but now our minds were on the Smithsons and as we walked soberly along we all turned in our saddles and looked across the lake to Charnworth House. It's not a tremendously large house, but it's very beautiful and still older than Nutsford. There is a long, low part with a battlemented roof and a gabled end with high gothic windows and stone-arched doorways. We gazed among the lawns and the dark, clipped hedges of yew for the Smithsons but there was no sign of them; not even a car by the front door.

"Perhaps they haven't come," said Cathy in disappointed voice.

"Dad said they'd be down today," observed Penny.

"We may be too early," I suggested, "perhaps even financial wizards have to be at their desks on Friday mornings."

"Yes, he'll roll up in his Rolls after an early lunch at the Ritz," said Penny.

"He may be the sort of billionaire who has ulcers and has to live on milk and pills," observed Cathy.

"And travels unobtrusively on a scooter," I suggested.

"With Mrs. Smithson dressed in fabulous furs riding pillion," giggled Cathy.

"Well, they're not there so we may as well have a canter," said Penny, urging Harlequin forward. And, making up for our earlier soberness, we all galloped madly to the gate by the church.

Since we could no longer treat Charnworth as though it belonged to us and take a short cut through the stable-yard to Castle Woods, we decided that we had better go for a ride on Charnworth Down. The ponies jogged along the back drive thinking they were going home and they were furious when we hurried them past Nutsford. They sulked when we took the Spayborne road and all up the steep track to the down. There is a lovely view in clear weather from the top of Charnworth Down; you can see the two great ranges of hills and the vale, a wide stretch of farmland between with the silver river winding through, and beyond that more hills. Sometimes we spend a long time looking at the view and Merlin and Jess always appear to take an artistic interest in it too, but now there wasn't one, the hills were dark shapes shrouded in a wet grey mist and the vale was blotted out by driving rain. The wind, blowing in gusty buffets, had excited the ponies out of their sulks and we sped along the track which circles the down. As we galloped, I forgot that Merlin was small and that I'd been looking forward to a larger horse. I gave myself up to the enjoyment of his long, low stride, to speed and the wind whistling by. I had forgotten how good it could feel. Presently Jess and Harlequin began to flag and we slowed up to a walk, but now we were riding into the wind and the rain lashed us, hard and cold, stinging our faces, forcing the ponies to lower their heads. They became eager to leave the hill and soon we were tearing down the track in a disorganised manner, the riders blinded by rain. In the valley it was warmer and it seemed very quiet without the wind roaring in our ears. We rode slowly home, stopping on the bridge to inspect the river; it was still quite low and flowing sluggishly; it takes a day or two for the rain falling in the hills to appear at Charnworth.

When we had rubbed down and fed the ponies we went into the house through the side door, which leads straight into the old kitchen. We were all feeling very healthy and infinitely superior to those who'd spent the morning indoors. Rory was still playing with the railway, but Andrew had evidently tired of it; he was lying on the floor reading the financial page of *The Times*.

"Steel is down again," he announced, "but Rubber and Zinc are up. Did you see him?"

"Mr. Smithson? No," I answered. "But we had a splendid ride."

"Oh curse the man! I do wish he'd turn up," said Andrew, removing himself and the paper from the floor. "Douglas, you'd better read this," he went on, proffering *The Times*. "He might not mind us being hopeless at maths if we know a bit about stocks and shares."

"Thanks," I said, "but if I've got to study high

finance the girls will jolly well have to do their bit and look lady-like."

"What a hope," said Andrew looking at them critically. "Cathy's not too bad, but Penny, you're wearing odd socks and, honestly, your hair."

Penny looked down at her socks, one green, one red, and said, "Well, someone's nicked their pairs. But anyway it didn't matter, we didn't meet them."

"Of course, they may ask us to tea," suggested Cathy suddenly. "After all, Lord Charnworth always had us to mince pies after the Carol Service."

"You mean, 'Christmas is the kiddies' time', and all that; a nice party with jellies and balloons," I said sarcastically.

"We might just as well eat jellies and play with balloons as rescue the fabulous furs or plunge into the lake," observed Penny. "I'd gladly be a lovable kiddy for one afternoon to get back Long Meadow for the ponies."

"They wouldn't think of Long Meadow," I told her. "They'd press expensive dollies on you. And anyway Rory's the only one who looks the least like a kiddy and he's not the sort to appeal to kiddy-lovers; he ought to be pudgy and dimpled."

We looked critically at Rory. His short sandy hair stands up in a curious way and looks like the bristles of an elderly toothbrush, he has the same sort of hard, wiry body as Penny and I and, somehow, he always manages to wear a defiant expression even when there is nothing to be defiant about.

"Might as well try to cuddle an alligator," I said.

"You're beastly," Cathy told me, "and I don't suppose you were any handsomer when you were eight with your huge great mouth."

"Well, I don't want to be cuddled by Mrs. S. mate,"
said Rory. "I bet she puts on tons and tons of ghastly
scent and simply stinks."

"I rather like scent," observed Andrew dreamily.

"Well, you can be the lovable kiddy then," Rory told
him, "instead of me."

At that moment there was a faint cry of "Will someone lay, please?" from the direction of the kitchen and
we looked at each other reluctantly.

"Rory and I laid breakfast," said Andrew in firm and
final tones so, groaning slightly, we older ones started
for the kitchen, shedding gloves and macintoshes on the
way. Not that I did any laying in the end because Mrs.
Toms who works for us occasionally when the spirit
moves her, or she is feeling poor, was there, giving, she
explained, the house a good turn-out for Christmas and
she wanted to remark on my startling growth and all
that sort of thing so we stood gossiping while the girls
laid.

Dad drove up in the Land-Rover at about one minute
to one and came in to lunch looking utterly dismal; he
slumped in his chair and avoiding Mum's anxious glance
began to serve. We all kept tactfully silent except for
asking each other to pass the salt in subdued tones, and
gradually it came out that the Smithsons *were* in
residence and that Dad had spent the morning with Mr.
Smithson. "We went through the estate balance sheets
for about the last five years, and I must say he's got the
most amazing grasp of figures I've ever known," Dad
told us. "He left me toiling behind. Well, that was all
right. But he'd got young Ross with him, you know, he's
in Bird and Thatcher the Spayborne auctioneers and

estate agents. Well, Ross seems to be acting as sort of general adviser; he's a smooth, glib sort; I don't like him and I don't think he likes me. Anyway, we got up to date on the accounts and we were working out the current capital depreciations. You know, every year the tractors are worth a bit less because they're older – all that sort of thing – then the dairy herd came up. Well, I know we *are* carrying a few old cows, but that's not going to bankrupt a place of this size, but I suppose it looks bad on paper; they eat the same as the others and don't produce as much. Anyhow they spotted it. And now we've got to weed out the unprofitable cows and that means Charnworth Carmen going to the next cattle sale."

"Not Carmen?" said Mum in horrified tones.

"Yes," Dad answered bitterly. "Three times champion of the Southern Counties Show and practically founder of the Charnworth herd. And look at the milk she's given in her time."

"But she won't fetch much, will she?" asked Mum.

"No, she'll be dogs' meat," said Dad. "And how I'm to tell Bill Martin, I don't know. He's always been so proud of that cow."

"Really, Mr. Smithson is wretched," said Mum. "Why does he have to start doing this sort of thing before he's been here two minutes?"

"Well, he's a business man," answered Dad, "and they're his cows." He sighed heavily. "I quite agree that the estate should be run in a business-like way, but poor old Carmen as dogs' meat! I suppose I'm sentimental," he added, pushing his half-eaten lunch away.

The thought of Carmen as dogs' meat was horrifying to all of us. The Charnworth dairy herd is stationed next

door to us on Home Farm and grazes the fields round
Nutsford. We all think Jerseys the beauties of the cow
world; with their dish faces and huge brown eyes they
seem like a cross between deer and Dartmoor ponies,
especially the heifers, and they appear so much more
intelligent than other cows. Mr. Martin, the head herdsman, had taught us all to milk and whenever we visited
him we were always shown Carmen and then her
daughters, of whom there were about eight.

Mum asked, "Can't you make him see that Carmen's
a sort of mascot, John?"

But Dad answered, "Look, they're his cows and with
young Ross announcing every ten seconds that a farm
should be judged like any other investment on the return
you're getting for your capital, how can I ask that
Charnworth Carmen be kept in honourable retirement?
They're business men, they don't see it like we do;
they'd think I was mad."

The thought of Carmen as dogs' meat was too much
for Rory and large tears began to splash into the gravy of
his Lancashire hot-pot.

"Oh Rory, don't," begged Mum. "Anyway Dad's
probably quite wrong; some nice person who just wants
a house cow will buy her and give her a lovely home."

"Besides," said Dad, in very unconvincing tones,
"Mr. Smithson may change his mind."

The subject was dropped hastily and for the rest of
lunch we talked in rather a forced way about Christmas.
But, when we'd washed up, we retired to the Old
Kitchen and as soon as we were out of earshot of our
parents we began to discuss Carmen again.

"We've *got* to do something," said Penny.

"Oh yes, we must," agreed Andrew. "Poor old

Carmen, she's such a nice cow."

"What on earth *can* we do?" I asked. "Get us a petition like people do for murderers? But that wouldn't be too popular with Dad."

Cathy said, "If she's only going as dogs' meat she wouldn't cost such a terrible lot, would she, Douglas?"

"No, I don't suppose so," I answered. "Jersey can't be sold as beef, can they? Not even stewing steak, they're a funny colour or something so they have to be dogs' meat. I imagine she'd fetch fifty to a hundred pounds, but I don't really know."

A gulping and snuffling noise from the sofa told us that we'd set Rory off. "I'm never going to eat hot-pot again," he announced defiantly, "and I'm not going to help make Storm's dinner either, I might be cutting up Carmen without knowing it," and he subsided in floods of tears.

"Oh, shut up, don't be such a cry baby." Penny spoke impatiently.

And Cathy said, "Rory, listen a minute, I've got a plan; why don't we find out which sale she's going to and then just go and buy her?"

We all gazed at Cathy. "Buy her?" I asked. "But what on earth should we do with her when we'd got her?"

"We could keep her at the Firs," said Cathy, "who'd obviously thought the whole thing out, "until we found her a good country home."

Penny's face lit up. "Yes, of course we could," she cried eagerly. "And sucks to old Smithson."

"Finance?" I said, endeavouring to be practical.

"Our post office accounts," answered Cathy. "It wouldn't be much between all of us – twenty pounds each if she cost a hundred. "

"It's an idea, " I said thoughtfully. "We'd have to keep it frightfully secret though. If it got around that we'd bought her it might make trouble between Dad and Mr. Smithson. "

"It wouldn't be difficult to keep her secret at the Firs, " Cathy pondered out loud, "the field's very sheltered and the spinney hides it from the road. "

"And Dad took up enough hay for the winter, " added Penny, "so he's not likely to go wandering round. "

"And the Gordon-Kellys are in South Africa until March, " said Cathy.

"That sounds all right, " I agreed. "But what I was really wondering was whether we can keep it a secret from Mum. If she knows she'll have to tell Dad and he'll probably have to tell Mr. Smithson and we shall all be in the soup. It isn't awfully easy to keep a secret like that and I can just hear Rory blurting it out when he and Mum are having a nice cosy good-night chat. "

"I won't, " said Rory, mopping his tears with the sleeve of his jersey. "I'm better at keeping secrets now. I never told Andrew that he was getting the electric train for his birthday and I knew about it for weeks. Do let's buy her; I've got forty-seven pounds, fifty pence in the post office. "

When we were young and people gave us money for birthday and Christmas presents Mum had always put it in the post office on the grounds that when we were older we would enjoy spending it on something sensible. For years it had seemed a very dull thing to do, but lately we'd begun to reverse the trend and in the summer Cathy had bought herself a pair of prize Silky bantams from which she proposed to breed a long like of champions, and I had taken myself on a week's sailing holiday. Now it looked as though Mum's efforts might save Carmen from the knacker. Cathy and I, who'd been given the safeguarding of our books, dashed upstairs to find them and Penny went to see if she could collect the other three from the drawer in the sitting-room where they lived with our birth certificates, Storm's pedigree and other official documents.

When we'd found them all we settled down to read the rules and regulations and it soon transpired that because the books were different ages they all gave different rulings on how much you could withdraw without notice.

"Supposing Cathy and I take out twenty-five pounds each and the rest of you twenty," I suggested, "that'll give us a hundred and ten which ought to be enough."

"Why should you and Cathy provide the most?" asked Penny.

"Because we're the eldest," I answered.

"I count as an older one now," said Penny, "and if I took out twenty-five too there would be a bit over to pay for her transport home."

"O.K.," I agreed. "After all we can easily put back what we don't spend."

Then we decided that we would visit the post office fairly soon and check up on the regulations, but that we would leave the collecting of the money until the last minute to minimise the dangers of losing it. We also decided that I should ask Dad, as casually as possible, what sale Carmen was going to. I felt very guilty about all these furtive arrangements and I was quite certain that it was irresponsible to encourage your younger brothers and sisters to take out their life's savings to buy a cow. But I comforted myself with the thought that at least our parents would approve of the cause, only it seemed a shame that we wouldn't be able to tell them that Carmen had been saved, not, at any rate, until we settled her in the good country home.

THREE

The second day of the holidays was wet, but not as wet. The rain fell in a grey, lifeless drizzle which was less wetting though more depressing than the squalls and torrents of the day before. Cathy and Penny announced at breakfast that it was still my turn to ride and that today I would be accompanied by Andrew on Harlequin and Rory on Jess.

"Oy, oy, oy!" I protested. "What about my nerves? Last time I saw Andrew ride Harlequin he was taken back to the Old Rectory at a brisk trot and I don't want to see Jess and Rory disappear in pursuit."

"Oh, I'll be all right," said Andrew, looking up from the book which he was reading surreptitiously under the table as he ate, "I can stop him most of the time."

"And I can canter," Rory boasted. "I've cantered at least twenty times I should think."

"They're all right," Penny told me firmly, "we've been taking them out every week-end all through the term; don't be such a fusspot."

"Okay," I answered. "I don't want to see the countryside littered with corpses, that's all." But privately I thought that it was going to be a pretty deadly ride.

Rory and I set off successfully, with only one slight uproar when Jess nipped Rory for tightening her girths roughly, but when we reached the Old Rectory we found that Andrew had failed to catch Harlequin. Looking like a Victorian orphan in Penny's beltless and buttonless macintosh, he was toiling round the muddy paddock after an equally muddy pony.

"He just won't be caught," wailed Andrew when he saw me at the gate. "I forgot to bring any oats or anything to catch him with and now he's furious."

"Well, of course he is," I shouted angrily, and began to search in my pockets for long forgotten titbits. Unfortunately Dad didn't seem to carry such things in his army surplus garment and my jodhs had been to the cleaners during the term. However, Rory produced a most revolting assortment from his mac – it had been Andrew's until the day before – he handed me a damp lump of sugar, two greenish-looking bits of bread and a half-sucked boiled sweet with a few oats adhering to it, and calling Andrew to hold Merlin, I went to catch Harlequin.

As soon as he saw my disgusting offerings he changed his tune. His ears shot forward and looking like a trade unionist who'd been standing up for his rights and got them, he came forward confidently. I took a firm hold of the bristly brush, which passed for his mane, before he tasted the titbits, but I needn't have bothered; he ate the lot with avidity.

We left the wet mud alone. Andrew showed an inclination to groom but since he is very slow and I had visions of our ride getting under way about half past two, I said firmly that brushing wet mud into the coat was the chief cause of mud fever and clapped on the saddle and bridle.

We mounted, and Merlin and I led the way through the village and past the South Lodge gates, ignoring Rory's pleas to ride on Charnworth Down.

"We're going in Castle Woods," I said firmly. I didn't relish pursuing runaway ponies all over the down. "There's a terrific canter through the woods, we can ford the brook. And we might meet Mr. Smithson," I added brightly, sounding rather like a travel agency advertisement. I didn't mention the fact that the only way home was by the road, for we could no longer take the short cut across country and anyway the stubble fields we'd galloped over in the summer were now sown with winter wheat. The thought of fording the brook contented Rory for the moment and Andrew was already submerged in dreams, so we proceeded peacefully until Harlequin suddenly realised that his rider wasn't of the same calibre as Penny. He stopped to graze on the grass verge, tearing at the coarse winter grass as though he hadn't been fed for months and ignoring Andrew's frantic tugs and kicks. Rory and I rode on for a bit hoping that Harlequin would follow and after a few moments he did; he thundered up the road at a brisk canter and then, when he was within a few yards of us, swerved to a sudden halt and began to graze again. Andrew shot up his neck and buried his face in the bristly mane.

"Give him a wallop," I instructed, riding on. But Harlequin continued to proceed in wild fits and starts and Andrew wailed that he'd forgotten his whip. Muttering angrily I turned back and lent him mine.

"Now come on," I said. "We're going to trot." It

had begun to rain harder and I turned up my collar and set off briskly. The clattering noises behind grew wilder. Harlequin was at the same game, but Andrew's wallops had livened things up, they now came up the road at the gallop and skidded violently to a halt when Harlequin saw a suitable patch of grass. Andrew was scarlet in the face and had lost both stirrups. "For goodness sake sit up, hang on to the reins and stop him doing that," I shouted. I was rapidly becoming exasperated.

"The reins keep slipping," answered Andrew in desperate tones and Harlequin, his ears flat back and his eyes rolling wickedly, continued to graze. I turned Merlin, who was becoming exasperated too, and rode back. I found that Andrew had no gloves on, his hands were blue with cold and, of course, it was impossible to get a grip on the wet reins.

"Where," I asked impatiently in the sort of voice school-masters use, "are your gloves?"

"I forgot them," said Andrew. I lent him one of mine and then with a hand on his reins I dragged Harlequin from the verge and led him beside Merlin. We trotted briskly along the road, past West Lodge and on up the hill until we reached the track into Castle Woods.

"Now," I said loosing Andrew, "you jolly well bully him. Don't be so weak. There's no grass here and in a minute we'll have a canter."

"About time too," said Rory. I ignored him and when we were round the corner and the long track lay straight ahead I cantered. After a few anxious looks behing me I decided that the ponies were going to behave and I began to enjoy myself. The fallen leaves made splendid going and Merlin's canter is smooth and rhythmic; soon my feelings of exasperation faded away.

We were nearly at the top of the woods where the track comes out at Castle Farm when I heard the whine of a portable power saw at work. Soon I could see it, right beside the track, and I slowed to a trot and yelled back, "Look out, horrifying object," just in case the earsplitting din had failed to penetrate Andrew's dreams. I intended to lead the way past at a brisk controlled trot, but at the last moment Merlin's courage failed him and he stopped dead with a snort and stood gazing at the saw with bulging eyes. Of course, Jess's and Harlequin's courage failed too. They stopped by bumping into Merlin. The woodmen were strangers, but they at once turned off the saw and approached with helpful expressions. As soon as the monster was silent, Merlin's courage returned and he rushed by at a canter. I looked round for my brothers. Unfortunately, Jess, who like Mrs. Guppy at the Lodge, believes that all strange men are thieves or murderers, had been approached by a woodman who wanted to lead her by and as he stretched out a hand to take her bridle, she turned and fled. Harlequin followed her and Andrew and Rory were both left lying on the leafy track. Swearing under my breath I rode back. The woodmen, seeing that no damage was done, were roaring with laughter and Rory was already running towards Jess who'd waited – she always does – a few yards down the track and was nibbling brambles. Of Harlequin there was no sign.

"Hell!" I said and then a horrible thought struck me. Harlequin knew the short cut home and he wouldn't care if the fields were sown or for the brittle feelings of a financial wizard.

"Hell and damn!" I said, thinking of the wet ground
and of a trail of hoofmarks across the winter wheat.
"Andrew, you lead Jess," I directed. Rory was already
scrambling into the saddle. "Don't let go of her whatever you do, and follow Harlequin's hoofmarks. I'll go
after him."

As soon as Andrew had a hand on Jess's reins, I set off
at a gallop. Except for the thought of what Dad was
going to say it was lovely to be galloping through the
woods in a really reckless manner. I came to the place
where the unofficial path led homeward and saw that
Harlequin's hoofmarks turned down it. Swearing about
brothers and borrowed ponies I took it too and urged
Merlin faster. Then I remembered that you could cut off
a sizeable corner by riding through one of the young
plantations; it was fenced and there was a wooden frame
and wire-netting gate at either end of the centre track
which I had sometimes jumped in happier times. I might
get ahead of Harlequin there I thought, but I hoped I
wouldn't bust the gates. Merlin cleared the first one
easily. I had a feeling that he was enjoying the chase
more than I was; he had no worries about Dad or winter
wheat. We took the second gate slowly and turned to
the right as we landed; almost at once we rejoined the
main track and my heart sank as I saw Harlequin's hoofmarks going on ahead. We've had it now, I thought, and
started to think of tactful sentences in which to tell Dad.
But then, as I came round the last corner before the
fields, I saw Harlequin coming towards me; on his back
he carried a strange boy. Merlin pulled up on his own
accord.

"Did you catch him before he got on the wheat?" I
asked breathlessly.

"I got him just down there," the boy turned and pointed. "He slowed up when he saw me; did someone fall off?"

"Yes, my brother," I answered. "Thanks for catching Harlequin," I went on. "I thought he was going to gallop the whole way home across the wheat and then there'd have been hell to pay."

"Does it hurt wheat to be galloped over?" asked the boy vaguely.

"Yes, especially in this weather." Then, as he showed no sign of dismounting I asked, "Would you like to ride Harlequin back?"

"Yes," he said, "until we find your brother."

"Come on, then, let's get out of here. This isn't the official bridlepath," I told him. As we rode along I took a quick look at the boy; he was, I decided, about my own size and age, though it was a little difficult to tell because he hadn't bothered to alter Andrew's stirrups and was riding with his knees practically under his chin. His hair and eyes were brown, his face very white and oddly inexpressive except for a wary look about the eyes.

"Are you O.K., I mean, can you ride?" I asked, letting Merlin, who was anxious to find Jess, break into a trot.

The boy nodded and since he seemed quite at home, even with Andrew's stirrups, I cantered on. Gradually we galloped. This time we skirted the plantation; Merlin seemed disappointed, but I didn't dare risk jumping the gates again, and then we came upon Andrew and Rory by the first of the gates; they were studying the ground with worried expressions on their faces and trying to make up their minds which set of hoofprints to follow.

"Oh thank *goodness,*" said Andrew in relieved tones when he saw Harlequin and then both he and Rory became speechless at the sight of the strange boy.

"He caught Harlequin," I explained. "*And* before he got on the winter wheat. By the way, what's your name?" I asked the boy.

"Nick," he answered. "Nick de Veriac."

"Well, I'm Douglas Conway," I told him. "And these are my brothers, Andrew and Rory."

Andrew said, "Thanks awfully for catching him."

"That's all right," answered Nick dismounting.

He stood watching us as Andrew climbed into the saddle; I thought he seemed envious and he was evidently at a loose end so, feeling grateful, I asked, "Would you like to try Merlin? We're going up through the woods to Castle Farm and I shall have to lead the ponies past the power saw which caused all the trouble or the same thing will happen again."

"Thanks," said Nick mounting with alacrity. With Jess in the lead and me at the rear we set off up the path. After a moment or two Andrew asked, "Would you like to ride Harlequin, Douglas?"

"No. I'm all right thanks," I answered. "I had a great gallop just now and jumped the plantation gates; Merlin's going marvellously."

"I hope the financial wizard wasn't lurking in the bushes," said Andrew.

"Well, he didn't leap out and say 'Trespassers will be prosecuted', or 'This is private property', so I don't think he was," I answered. And then, as the banshee howls of the power saw were growing louder, I took a firm hold of both ponies. I didn't have to bother about

Nick because I could see that he was quite at home on Merlin; he rode casually with one hand on the reins and he seemed to sit very loosely in the saddle, but he looked confident and experienced. As soon as the woodmen caught sight of us they silenced the saw and began to shout encouraging remarks. "Ride 'em cowboy!" and "Sit tight this time," but I was too taken up with hanging on to the jostling, jogging ponies to think of a reply. We got past safely, except that Harlequin trod on one of my feet, and then, when I had loosed my brothers I suggested that they should all canter on to Castle Farm and wait for me there; it seemed a waste to walk on such a splendid stretch of track.

They agreed enthusiastically and shot off at speed, but I knew that Jess and Harlequin would both be trotting long before they reached the top of the track which becomes more and more uphill.

When I caught up with them Andrew and Rory were both chattering madly, "We've shown Nick the ruins," Andrew told me, "but we didn't go too near in case the financial wizard was lurking."

"Blow him," said Rory. "Come on, where's this brook?" I opened a gate and led the way down a track to the ford and we all waited patiently while Jess did her usual Mrs. Guppyish act of testing the depth of the water – she paws anxiously before she takes each step even though she must know by now that the brook is never more than two feet deep.

When they were all across, Andrew dismounted and Nick led Harlequin back for me. I was beginning to wonder when Nick was going home so I explained that we were going back to Charnworth along the road and asked if that was the right direction for him.

"Yes, more or less," he answered.

"Whereabouts do you live then?" I asked.

"London mostly," he said, "I'm staying here with friends because my parents are abroad."

I was going to ask where the friends lived, but my remark about going home by the road had just sunk in and Andrew and Rory set up a wail.

"Oh, Douglas, you can't make us, not *all* the way along the road; it's cruelty to brothers," protested Andrew reproachfully.

"It's the only way," I told him. "We can't take unofficial short cuts now."

"Oh, well, I suppose we shall survive. You can keep Harlequin for a bit if you like; I'll walk."

Rory wasn't so stoical. "Bother that dreary, lousy, wretched old Smithson," he stormed. "He's mucking everything up. I'd like to . . ."

"Shut up," I roared at him. For not only was Nick a stranger, but we were on the Charnworth estate and Rory's voice carries. The last thing I wanted was for us to make things more difficult for Dad.

"It isn't Mr. Smithson's fault for coming, it's Lord Charnworth's for dying," observed Andrew, "changes are always beastly."

"And it won't kill you to do some road work, you can practise riding properly and then perhaps you won't fall off *every* time the ponies swerve," I said disagreeably.

There was a long silence after this until Nick announced that it was his turn to walk and offered me Merlin. But, feeling rather remorseful, I told Andrew that he could have him.

Andrew mounted and rode along proudly and I must say he looked much better on Merlin than he had on

Harlequin. He doesn't seem to be much use at making obstinate ponies behave; they always bully him. Penny is the opposite, she'd rather ride a badly behaved pony than a perfectly schooled one. Cathy likes them well-schooled and I'm sort of in between. I hate refusers and boring animals that won't go where you want them to, but I shouldn't want something so perfectly schooled that I felt I was unschooling it all the time.

Nick showed no sign of taking himself off so we went on swopping ponies and taking it in turns to walk until we reached our lane. Then Nick asked if it was all right for him to come in, and of course we said yes. He helped us to water and feed the ponies and when Cathy and Penny appeared, rather floury because they'd been cooking, we introduced them. Cathy took him to see the bantams and Andrew took him to see the electric train and then he said very reluctantly that he supposed he had better go and what were we going to do that afternoon?

We explained that we were Christmas shopping in Spayborne. Nick stood looking more and more dismal until at last Cathy took pity on him and said that it was Penny's and her turn to ride tomorrow and if Nick liked to come she would squeeze herself on Jess and Penny wanted to ride Harlequin because she was schooling him. Nick accepted gladly and hurried off with a much more cheerful expression. When he was safely out of earshot I said, "It looks as though we've got him for the rest of the holidays."

"Don't be beastly," objected Cathy. "Anyway, he seems nice."

"Yes, I think he's all right," I agreed. "Not very talkative."

"He talked to us as Castle Farm," said Andrew. "He

said his father was in the secret service and he thinks his mother's gone to France to join him, but he doesn't really know. I wish we had some exciting relations."

FOUR

Nick was forgotten at lunch because Dad had come straight from another session with Mr. Smithson and seemed full of indignation.

"Broilers!" he said, chopping angrily at the beef-steak-pie. "Broilers! He might as well start a sausage factory at Charnworth and have done with it. Of course it was Ross who put him up to it; I'm beginning to wonder whether he isn't hoping to step into my shoes."

"*Oh no,*" said Mum, "not after all the business you've given Bird and Thatcher."

"I daresay he's getting tired of being their assistant and thinks this would be a nice light job with plenty of perks." Dad spoke bitterly.

"But he's no practical experience of farming, has he?" asked Mum spooning out brussels sprouts.

"I've no idea," said Dad. "He sets himself up as a great authority, gives Mr. Smithson pompous little lectures on everything from the Rent Act to calf-rearing and half the time he's talking through his hat. But it's his oily manner I can't stand, still I shook him out of it this morning."

"What happened?" asked Mum, beginning to eat.

"Well, they came down to my office and we discussed one or two outstanding repairs and the empty cottage at Ashmoor and then Mr. Smithson brought up the subject of broilers, asked what I thought of putting up a dozen houses and cashing in on the market while it was still good. I pointed out that he'd have to get planning permission to put up the houses and pay rates on them and he said yes, he realised that, but what did I think of the idea? I said I thought it was a goddam awful idea and that it was one thing for some poor devil of a smallholder, who was trying to eke out a living from a few acres of useless land, to go in for them, but to start mass production of caged and antibiotic-fed birds at Charnworth – the wretched animals never see the light of day and they even come to be killed hanging upside down from a conveyor belt. Well, I told him that if you've got to do it for a living, you've got to, but in my opinion it wasn't farming.

"Then Ross chipped in; he said that it *was* farming, that my attitude was out of date and that food production was becoming a scientific industry – the days of leaning on gates in the sunshine and prodding pigs were over. A farm could only be judged on the profit it made per ratio of invested capital. I blew up and said a lot of things I've been wanting to say for these last two days and then he lost his temper and we were both shouting our heads off."

"What on earth did Mr. Smithson say?" asked Mum looking faintly alarmed.

"Oh, he just sat there with an inscrutable expression and let us get on with it," answered Dad, wolfing beefsteak-pie.

I waited until things had calmed down a bit and

pudding – frozen raspberries and Jersey cream – was well under way. Then, keeping my voice as casual as possible, I asked my question. "Dad, is Carmen really going?" I asked. "I mean have you settled what sale you're sending her to?"

"We have," he answered, looking rather as though I'd kicked him on the shin. "She's going to the Jersey sale in Charlbury next Monday," and pushing away the remains of his pudding he got up and walked out of the room.

"Oh Douglas," said Mum reproachfully, and I could see that she was thinking that I was heartless as well as irresponsible, but I didn't attempt an explanation. I was far too busy wondering what possible reason we could produce for going to Charlbury.

We washed up in our most speedy manner, with only one casualty – it was cracked already – and then there was a mad rush to get ready for Spayborne. Changing was complicated by hasty discussions between Cathy, Penny and myself on reasons for going to Charlbury, and Andrew's and Rory's desire to know what we wanted for Christmas and to tell us what they wanted in return.

Charlbury is the cathedral city and capital of the county; it lies about eighteen miles to the north-west of Charnworth and when we go there we usually make a family outing of it and have a grand lunch at the Rose and Crown or go to the theatre.

"We could make out we had to go to get Mum's or Dad's present, I suppose," suggested Cathy. "It sounds a bit mean, but we've got to do something. The morning bus goes from the post office at half past nine."

"Mum might be persuaded to let you and me go," I

said, "but I don't know about the others."

"Oh, we *must* all go," protested Andrew.

"Let's simply say we can't get what we want in Spayborne," suggested Penny. "After all, it's true, we can't buy Carmen there if she's being sold in Charlbury." She began to giggle.

"Oh shut up," I told her, "it isn't funny."

I was beginning to wish that I felt a bit more irresponsible instead of weighed down with a dismal feeling that Monday was awfully soon and that things were getting out of control.

"We're to say that we can't get what we want in Spayborne then?" asked Andrew.

"Yes, I suppose it's as good a reason as any other," I answered dismally. And then hearing Mum calling us to hurry, I went to change.

When at last we all appeared at the garage Mum looked at us critically and announced that Rory had half his lunch on his face and that she drew the line at Penny wearing *such* odd socks; Rory produced his handkerchief and said that he'd wash in spit, he *couldn't* go all upstairs again. And Penny protested that she'd looked *everywhere* and that the other sock in each pair had absolutely gone. "Well, go and put on a pair of Andrew's school ones then," said Mum, trying to sound patient, "and for goodness sake hurry up."

Penny stumped off muttering and Rory tried to stir Andrew into objecting to lending his socks, but he was deep in thought over his Christmas list and refused to bother. "She can have them all," he said, "they're only beastly old school ones. Cathy, what do *you* want?"

Rory elected to sit on my knee, which is hell because he can't sit still and he's very bony, but the car, which is Mum's own and doesn't belong to the estate like the Land-Rover, is a baby one and not really big enough to hold all of us, so someone has to sit on someone and at least Rory is a couple of stone lighter than Andrew.

"I've got four pounds, sixty-seven pence," announced Rory, as we drove towards Spayborne. " Divided by six that's more than seventy pence for each person, so you're all going to get terrific presents from me this year."

Andrew, who'd been feeling nervously in his pockets, said, "I think I've lost my money."

"Oh *no*," cried Mum in despairing tomes. "Andrew, you lose your money every Christmas."

Penny said, "You can't have lost all of it because it wasn't in a purse. You've probably just left it behind."

And Cathy, observing as I had, that Andrew's face was turning ominously red, asked, "Are you sure it's lost? Here, let me look." And she and Penny started turning out his pockets.

Suddenly Andrew gave a cry of joy. "It's all right," he said, "I've remembered," and extracted the money from the breast pocket of his jacket. "I thought it would be safer there," he·explained.

"You're a nut case, mate," shrieked Rory, bouncing and digging his bones into me.

Penny began the build-up for Charlbury. "I do wish Spayborne was just a bit bigger," she said in dissatisfied tones, "or that it just had *one* decent shop. Really Elijah N. Briggs is terribly behind the times."

"Windows full of aprons and tea-cosies," agreed Cathy, "and the dreariest clothes."

"The toy shop's pretty lousy too," said Andrew with a heavy sigh.

"And there isn't even a Woolworths," complained

Rory. Mum was looking extremely startled and I began to shake with suppressed laughter.

"None o' that, mate," said Rory giving me a sharp dig with a bony elbow.

"The bookshop never has a single book you want," Penny went on, "and there won't be time to order things for Christmas."

"You are becoming a horrid blasé lot," said Mum. "You'd better go and live in Birmingham. And what about the china shop? You used to love going in there."

I said, "Time passes; the little chicks grow up, take wing. . . ."

And Cathy pointed out, "We can't go on giving each other china horses for ever."

Thinking that perhaps we were overdoing it a bit, I changed the subject. "What does Dad want for Christmas?" I asked.

"Oh, all the usual things," Mum answered vaguely.

"I thought we might join up this year and get him something decent," I said, looking round at the others.

"Count me out, mate," said Rory, bouncing. "I'm going to give all my presents on my own this year."

"Do you think he would like a large posh torch?" I asked. "I saw some red ones in a shop somewhere which weren't *too* expensive. I think we could afford one even without Rory."

"I should think he'd love one," answered Mum.

"We could go and look at them," said Andrew, not wishing to commit himself.

"I don't suppose there are any in Spayborne," remarked Penny scornfully.

"Otherwise there's tools and books and ties," I went on thoughtfully, "but I think he's gone off carpentry and I don't think he likes our taste in ties. He hasn't worn the one we gave him last year since Boxing Day, has he, Cathy?"

"No, not once," Cathy agreed. "I suppose he thinks midnight blue and yellow a bit flash."

"If we'd bought the one we really likes – the one with notes of music on it – he wouldn't have worn it on Boxing Day," I observed.

"Darling, do shut up and see if I'm going to hit that car." said Mum crossly and I became aware that she was trying to back into the last parking space left in Spayborne. "No, you're all right," I answered, "go on."

We climbed out, stiff from being squashed, and began to make plans.

"Rory, you're coming with me," said Mum, sounding quite convincingly firm.

"Oh no," wailed Rory. "Hw can I buy your present if you're *there*? And anyway I bet you're going to do boring shopping and I want to go to the china shop – "

"Don't whine," I said, pushing him.

And then, as usual, Cathy offered. "I'll have him some of the time if you like, Mum. Only I've got to buy his present."

"All right then, you have him first," said Mum. "Look, supposing we meet here in three-quarters of an hour and see how much more you've all got left to do?"

We agreed to that, those of us who had watches looked at them, and then we set off in a mad dash for the china shop. We spent ages there, just looking. Making my way steadily around the shelves I saw the Italian jug. It was quite tall, rather a fabulous shape and painted in wonderful colours, just the sort of thing that Mum liked. I thought, but the price ticket told me that I was going to need several sharers.

I collected Cathy and Penny. Cathy agreed that it was perfect and said that Mum was always grumbling that she hadn't a decent jug in which to arrange catkins and things, but I could see from Penny's face that she thought a jam-jar would really do just as well. Leaving Cathy to convince her I found Andrew who was dithering over china horses. "Which do you think Cathy would like?" he asked in a loud whisper.

"Neither," I said firmly. "She's tired of them. Come and look at this jug."

Andrew couldn't make up his mind about the jug and Penny was wavering too, so finally, in exasperation, Cathy and I marched them out of the china shop and across the market-place to the ironmongers, agreeing between ourselves to take them back later for another look.

It was just the same in the ironmongers. Andrew dithered over the most efficient red and chromium torch which could be switched to a spotlight or not as desired. More exasperated still, Cathy and I whirled them to men's outfitters windows, to the chemist, and then to Elijah N. Briggs, who had egg-cosies as well as tea-cosies in his window. Rory had bought bath-salts for Mum in the chemist's but Andrew and Penny had continued to dither. At last, quite cheerfully, they agreed both to the torch and the Italian jug. Then we sent them off on their own and, with Rory between us, we dashed to the book shop where we bought Penny the latest work by her favourite pony-book writer. Cathy and I generally give our presents together because you can afford better ones. While we were choosing the book Rory wandered off to the gift department and and bought Penny a tartan purse – privately I thought it was awful but Rory was delighted with it so I kept quiet.

We visited the toy shop next and had to wait outside because Andrew and Penny were inside and every time we opened the door, they yelled, "Get out, secret," and "If you look we won't give you any presents," and other dire threats. By the time they'd gone and Rory had had practically every electric train accessory in the shop unpacked and finally bought Andrew a buffer-stop, three milk-churns and a porter and Cathy and I had bought him a horse-box and a fish-van, we were all in a state of nervous collapse and nearly an hour had gone by. We ran madly to the car. Mum took Rory and announced that we could only have another twenty minutes, so, uttering frantic cries, we set out again. Cathy agreed to share in giving Rory a new book by his favourite author, which we'd noticed in the bookshop, but not dared to buy as he was there. She said that she would get it. I gave her my share of the money and set off up the street. Then I found that Andrew was with me.

"Please come and help," he said. "I just can't decide which to give Penny." I went back to the ironmongers with him and, after much hesitation, we chose Penny a knife, and then he came with me across to the china shop. I should think the shop owner felt like screaming at the sight of us. I bought Cathy a picture of a horse, which I had seen her admiring earlier. It was by a Chinese artist and so jolly expensive that it took all the rest of my money and reduced me to the undignified position of borrowing one pound, eighty from Andrew. Then I gave a cry of relief and headed for the car. We were all snugly packed in with our presents when Mum and Rory appeared.

"Finished?" she asked in rather unbelieving tones.

"Yes, I've had a brilliant shop," I answered smugly.

"So have I," said Andrew.

Penny gave us a furious look. "We've all done except for one thing," she said, "and we can't get it here."

Andrew and I lost our self-satisfied expressions.

"Oh yes," we agreed, "except for *that.*"

"Oh, bother, what is it?" asked Mum.

"Secret," we all cried at once.

"Well, can't you get something else?"

"No," we shook our heads sadly.

"Well, don't just sit there, for goodness' sake go and look for whatever it is," said Mum, who'd plainly had enough.

"But we've tried simply *everywhere,*" protested Penny. "There simply weren't any in Spayborne."

"We'll have to go to Charlbury," I said. "There's bound to be one there; Cathy and I can go on the bus."

"Yes, good idea," agreed Cathy in slightly unnatural tones.

Mum sighed. "Here, doughnuts to eat now," she said, handing me a paper bag as she got in.

We all revived as we ate our doughnuts, except for Rory who didn't need reviving, but bounced ceaselessly and would whisper to each of us in turn what he was giving everyone else. When your present was being mentioned he expected you to block your ears and make a loud humming noise so that you couldn't possibly hear what he said.

He'd got about half-way through when Mum announced that if there was any more humming she'd go mad and there wouldn't be a Christmas dinner if she was in a mental hospital.

FIVE

On Saturday, which was actually fine, Nick appeared early. He wouldn't come into the house, but lurked in the stable while we did dreary tasks like making our beds, or rather masking their unmade states with neatly arranged counterpanes. The neat arrangement takes just as long as making the bed properly but is, somehow, more satisfactory.

We were all hoping that Nick was working too, we imagined him grooming industriously, but when we went out to the stable we found him sitting on a bale of straw, smoking a cigarette in a self-conscious manner, and the ponies still caked in mud.

Andrew and Rory gazed at him in wide-eyed admiration, and I said, "For Heaven's sake, Nick, not in a stable."

"Sorry," he stamped out the cigarette hastily. "Don't you smoke, Douglas?" he asked.

"Yes, of course I do sometimes at school," I answered impatiently. I wasn't going to admit that I didn't like the taste. "But it's a bit of an expensive habit and I can't afford it," I added.

Penny changed the subject. "Why on earth didn't you groom," she asked, "instead of just sitting there?"

groom," she asked, "instead of just sitting there?"

Nick, who was beginning to look very crushed and miserable, explained that he didn't know how to groom and, feeling that I'd been a bit pompous over the smoking, I offered to teach him. While Penny went for Harlequin, Cathy and Rory groomed Jess, and Andrew and I taught Nick, not only how to groom, but to saddle and bridle as well.

With such a large labour force the ponies were ready in record time and we explained our plans to Nick. We had to go to the post office and we were going to collect Penny and Harlequin on the way back and then go to the field at the Firs to ride; and the horseless people were to organise a course of jumps. We decided that we might as well patrol the park on the way to the post office, so, with Nick on Merlin and Rory on Jess – Cathy, who is very weak about standing up for her rights had let him pinch some of her turn – we walked up the back drive to the church and took the path across the park.

Nick couldn't make out the purpose of the patrol and he seemed so worried I had to explain about our hope that the financial wizard would fall in the lake, whereupon we would all plunge to his rescue and how, with a choke in his voice, he was to swear eternal gratitude and offer us Long Meadow for the ponies.

Nick seemed to think it rather a mad idea, and I admitted that I agreed with him.

"But what *can* you do for financial wizards?" I asked, "except rescue them from untimely ends and prevent their wives' fabulous furs or the Charnworth Gainsborough from being stolen?"

"Can't imagine," said Nick unhelpfully, and "Can we have a canter?"

Cathy said yes, but that it must be a slow one as the park is one of Rory's falling-off places.

The sun was shining weakly as we came out of Home Farm Spinney and into the village, and the sky was clearing, gradually becoming more and more blue. The others said they were going to sun themselves and sent me into the post office alone. Mr. and Mrs. Dent, old Mrs. Bone and the retired blacksmith, Mr. Crabbe, were all talking at once, but when they saw me they stopped abruptly so I guessed they were talking about what are known locally as the "Changes". Mrs. Dent said it was a nice morning but wouldn't last and I explained about drawing the money out of five different accounts on Monday. "Christmas, I suppose, dear," she said. "Well, you needn't have worried to call in, that rule's been changed, dear, it's one hundred pounds now, but I'll have it all ready for you." And then old Mrs. Bone asked, "And what does your Dad think of all they changes up the 'ouse?"

"Too early to say yet," I answered, hoping I wasn't going to be pumped.

"We heard," Mr. Dent looked at me darkly, "we heard that things weren't going too well."

"Well, things are bound to be a bit tricky ar first," I answered, "I mean we've had Charnworth here for getting on for a thousand years, haven't we? The first Charnworth is supposed to have come over with William the Conqueror."

"It doesn't seem right to me," said Mrs. Dent, "taking Lord Charnworth's money away in death duties, and yet there's Mr. Smithson got any amount."

"Came round to my place yesterday, 'e did." Mrs. Bone is deaf and speaks in a loud, hoarse voice. "'What, no central heating Mrs. Bone?' 'e said. 'We'll 'ave to see about that.' 'Mr. Smith,' I said, 'I've lived 'ere forty-two years next April and I've never 'ad no central heating and I don't want no changes now.' Told 'im straight I did, 'Mr. Smith,' I said – "

"Put central heating in and up goes the rent," stated Mr. Crabbe gloomily. "Look at them council 'ouses at 'Arley Cross; exorbitant, they are."

"I do hear he's thinking of building a factory out at Ashmore," said Mr. Dent.

While they were all talking I quietly escaped.

"You've been *ages*," said Penny, who'd evidently ridden down from the Old Rectory.

Cathy asked, "Did you have to fill in masses of forms?"

"No," I answered, "I was being pumped for Dad's opinion of the financial wizard. We shall have to beware." I looked at Andrew and Rory, "If you get asked, you don't know a thing."

"Mrs. Browne had a go at me," Penny told us as we set off up the road. "She appeared when I was grooming and wanted to know what the F.W. was like and whether Mum had met Mrs. F.W. yet. She wants to call on them but her husband won't let her, he says he can't afford to entertain billionaires. She went on and on, you know how she does. That's why I came down to the post office, I couldn't stand it any longer."

"What did you tell her?" I asked.

"Nothing really. I looked as goofy as possible and said that Dad thought him a very clever man. Didn't Dad say he had a remarkable grasp of facts or figures or something?"

"Yes," I agreed. Cathy stopped and began to giggle

weakly. She's an awful giggler.

"None of that," I told her, and Andrew and I each took an arm and tried to push her along. Nick said, "I forgot, I wanted to buy something at the post office. Would you like to put that floppy female on Merlin? I'll run back and then catch you up."

"Oh honestly, Nick, you're cracked," said Penny. "You've been sitting outside for hours. Why didn't you go in then?"

"Shan't be long, you go on," answered Nick dismounting. We put Cathy on Merlin and I made Rory give Jess to Andrew; unless you look out Rory's turn is an endless affair. He never suggests that it's over. I know he's only eight, but I don't see that it kills him to walk occasionally. I suspect that when I'm at school he hogs everything because Andrew is usually too deep in dreams to notice and Cathy is too good-natured to object, only Penny and I try to keep him in order.

We told the horsemen to ride on and Rory and I crossed the river and climbed the hill in a leisurely manner, giving Nick a chance to catch up. He appeared breathless and laden with paper bags just as we reached the Firs. The field is a big one, about six acres and very flat; it would be cold and windswept for it is right on the top of Sutton's Hill, but two dark spinneys planted to the north and east shelter it from the worst of the winds. There is a large and useful open shed in the field which was half full of hay brought up by Dad to last the ponies through the winter.

The horsemen were already dragging hurdles from the shed and when we joined them Cathy said, "It'll have to be cross-country, Douglas. Dad didn't bring up the gate and wall, they're in the Stone Barn; there's only a few poles and oil-drums."

The gate and wall are not as grand as they sound; they are rather rickety affairs made by me and look all right from a distance as we concealed their blemishes under several good thick coats of paint.

"Oh well, there's plenty of brushwood in the spinneys and with Nick to help I should think we could get that old chicken-house into position. Then there's the water-trough. We can make quite a decent course," I answered.

"I do wish there was a brook up here and a few hills," said Penny in dissatisfied tones. "If only the F.W. had some horsey children," she sighed. "*Think* of making a cross-country course in Castle Woods."

We thought of it. "At least three water splashes," said Cathy.

"And plenty of stones by the Castle for a stone wall, and a really great slide down from the Castle," suggested Andrew.

"There's even a ready-made quarry," I added. "Still," I pointed out, "the F.W.'s children would probably be too grand for us; they'd have horse-boxes and grooms and ride at 'The Horse of the Year Show'."

"They'd wear navy blue coats with velvet collars and their horses would be clipped," agreed Cathy.

"And if they fell off and got dirty, they'd cry," added Rory.

We stood looking at the hurdles, the poles and our six rather battered oil-drums and we felt dissatisfied now that we'd allowed ourselves to covet Castle Wood.

"Oh well," I said, "Come on, non-riders to work."

"Have a sweet first," suggested Nick, putting the bags he'd been carrying on an oil-drum and adding more and more from his pockets.

"Great," Rory threw himself upon them and, opening them greedily, revealed almost every sort of sweet and chocolate the post office kept. "Nick! You must have spent *pounds*!" exclaimed Andrew.

"I've got plenty more," said Nick, and producing an elegant wallet he showed us a roll of notes. "My father sent it to me."

Andrew gasped obligingly. "You are lucky," and "You mind it doesn't get nicked, Nick," said Rory falling about with laughter at his joke.

"I can protect myself," said Nick producing a sheath-knife from his belt. "I should think you could kill someone with this."

Andrew and Rory examined it enviously. Cathy, Penny and I looked at each other. We had no intention of being impressed.

"Nick," I said, "do you want to ride? Because if so, take this horse." I looked at the girls. "Why don't you have a four-corners race while we organise the jumps?" I suggested.

"Oh yes, do let's, we haven't had one for ages," Penny sounded enthusiastic. Nick mounted without a word and the girls began to explain the race to him; we started work on the course.

We watched the race, which entails touching some object in each corner of the field as we piled oil-drums, carried poles and dragged brushwood from the spinney. Merlin, who had give the smaller ponies a short start, failed to catch them; Penny won. She very often does, as she is much more competitive than the rest of us. I have to ride absolutely flat out when I race against her, otherwise there are irritating cries of "Penny has *even* beaten *Douglas*."

Rory held the ponies while they got their second winds and the rest of us got the old chicken-house, a dilapidated ark, into position. It collapsed completely when we moved it and was really no more than a pile of wood, but it made something to jump.

Then we explained the course to the riders and, except for some wails about the water-trough, they agreed that it was a nice one, especially the jump into the spinney – we'd taken down a strand of wire and filled the gap up with brushwood – and the hay bale in and out.

We sent Cathy first and except for a refusal at the water-trough and a run-out at the chicken-house she was clear. Harlequin was eliminated for three refusals at the water-trough, but, when Jess provided a lead, he jumped it and then went on to finish the course.

Nick had assured us that he could jump, but from the way he rode round the course we knew he wasn't very experienced. He galloped absolutely flat out at everything, but luckily Merlin, who is a very good jumper, steadied himself. They had a run-out at the water-trough, through going too fast, and they got completely lost in the spinney, where Nick scratched his face on a bough; he emerged dripping with blood.

While Cathy organised first aid by lending Nick a cleanish handkerchief and directing whereabouts to mop, Penny suggested that I rode Merlin round. She said that it would do Harlequin good to go again and she wanted a lead. Since Nick's bloody face had put Andrew and Rory off a bit and they'd stopped demanding a turn round the whole course each, which our nerves and Jess's wind would hardly have survived, I didn't have to say that the ponies were tired and must be taken home forthwith, but mounted gladly.

Merlin jumped splendidly and I found myself wishing for real fences a foot or so higher. Harlequin went much better with a lead, though he knocked down the oil-drum jump.

Then Andrew had a go on Jess and we let him do everything but the spinney and the water-trough and afterwards Rory jumped some poles on oil-drums; he really isn't safe over anything else. Finally we put Nick back on Merlin and explained how one is supposed to sit and hold the reins and then we made him jump from a trot instead of a flat-out gallop. He took it all in very good part, even being instructed by five people at once, and he got the idea very quickly. When we told him that he was now quite respectable and no longer a public danger he looked terribly pleased. Then as lunch-time was rapidly approaching we shoved the hay bales and hurdles back into the shed and set off for home; a mixed party of walkers and riders all eating Nick's sweets.

SIX

At lunch I told Dad how Penny had been grilled by Mrs. Browne and I by the village. I told him about Mrs. Bone's central heating and the factory at Ashmoor but not about the rather dismal rumour that "things" weren't going too well.

"It's like that all over the estate," said Dad with a sigh. "Some of the stories going round are quite incredible. Yesterday Colonel Barrett telephoned me from Harley Cross and said the whole village was in a ferment because Mr. Smithson was supposed to be going to build nineteen bungalows on the football field. This morning the Vicar stopped me and asked if it was true that Forest Hill was to be drilled for oil. Whichever of our farms I visit I hear the most startling reports about what's happening on the other four, and the twenty-odd tenant farmers are all counting their savings and shivering in their shoes.

"There's not much I can do about it. Whenever I can shake off Mr. Smithson I go round trying to calm everyone down, but no sooner is my back turned, than a new rumour starts."

"Of course people are a bit unreasonable," said

Mum. "Why couldn't Mrs. Bone accept the central heating gracefully? If he offers it to us John the answer is a delighted 'yes' and you can mention that another bathroom and a downstairs cloakroom would be a distinct improvement.

"He's very shocked by the lack of Mod. Cons. in the village," Dad went on, "and he didn't believe me when I said that his modernisation plans wouldn't please everyone. I told him that we'd better begin on the younger peoples' cottages and then we might get some converts among the older generation. I suppose he thought he'd find out if I was right and tackled Mrs. Bone. Still, he does seem to want to do his best for the village, and that's something."

"Doesn't he even believe what you tell him?" asked Mum.

"No, he verifies everything. He asks Ross or his lawyer or a friend in the Ministry of Agriculture or just finds out for himself. He's most exhaustingly thorough, but I suppose these successful business men are. Still, this morning he asked me what Lord Charnworth has done about the employees at Christmas and when I told him that the men with families always had turkeys and everyone else chickens he said that he'd like things to go on as usual, but would I let him have a list of those who have presents."

"I bet we don't appear on the list this year," said Mum.

"No," Dad admitted, "we don't. I'll get our turkey in Spayborne."

Later, Cathy and I cornered Mum and asked if it was all right for us to go to Charlbury on Monday. We'd arranged with the others that, as we were the most likely to be allowed to go, we should get a definite yes first and then they could all pester to be allowed to come too as much as they liked. At first Mum said it was idiotic to go eighteen miles to Charlbury for one thing, and anyway, what was this mysterious thing? We were driven into pretending that it was her Christmas present and then she thought a visit to Charlbury all the more unnecessary. "But Spayborne's full of things I'd love," she protested. "I'll make a list of helpful suggestions if you're really stuck; I can think of several things I'd like from the post office. There's absolutely no need to go to Charlbury."

Cathy and I looked at each other in despair, and then tried a different tack. We pointed out that we were now awfully old and ought to be allowed to go to Charlbury if we wanted to and finally we admitted to a desire to walk round the shops – an occupation which Mum has always despised.

"It isn't that I mind you going," said Mum, giving way at last, "I mean if you had a sensible reason. It just seems mad to me to spend three hours in the bus when you could be riding. Still, I suppose if we do have to leave Nutsford and live in a flat somewhere, you'll all be perfectly happy walking round Woolworths."

I gave up; it's hopeless to argue with parents when they're in that sort of mood, especially when you can't admit the real reason for your strange desire. But as I went out of the room saying that it was my turn to take the ponies back to the Firs, I heard Cathy pointing out that because a person wanted to go shopping in Charlbury once a year at Christmas it didn't mean to say that she'd like to live in a flat for the rest of her life.

On Sundays in the holidays we usually give the ponies

a rest. It seemed rather a waste to give them a rest on this Sunday as it looked as though they might get one on Monday too, but as we didn't know how many of us were going to Charlbury it was difficult to make plans.

Penny, Andrew and Rory were all set to pester Mum from an early hour, but at eight o'clock Dad appeared and said that as Mum seemed tired he'd persuaded her to stay in bed for a bit, and would we help him get things under way?

It was Cathy's and Andrew's turn to feed the ponies so they rushed off to the Firs and the rest of us started work on breakfast. We had two frying-pans in action and fried everything we could find, including masses of bread. Except for Penny falling over Storm and smashing an egg, the milk boiling over and two pieces of toast having to be written off, everything went well and Penny carried a substantial breakfast up to Mum.

Later, when we'd finished stuffing ourselves Dad said he thought it would be nice if he took us all to church and there was a wild rush to get everything done. Dad dealt with the Aga, the boiler and the fire, because he's good with them, Cathy washed up assisted by Andrew and Rory, Penny and I removed the outsides from a multitude of brussels sprouts. Penny kept grumbling that I was slow and I retaliated by saying her methods were inefficient and pointing out mucky leaves, foreign bodies and things which might be caterpillars left behind in her haste.

By the time we'd all got knives and done the potatoes the kitchen looked as though a tornado had struck it; there was about an inch of water on the floor and bits of sprout and potato everywhere. We mopped and swept energetically, but it still looked pretty deadly when we dashed upstairs to make ourselves presentable for church.

Our vicar copes with three parishes, Charnworth, Shilling Manford and Harley Cross and we were disappointed when Dad, after consulting the parish magazine, announced that it was the week for Morning Service to be held at Shilling Manford; we'd been hoping for Charnworth and a glimpse of the F.W.; we thought it would be difficult for him not to go to church when the bell called him from his own garden.

When we got back Mum was up. She said she'd had the most wonderful lazy morning and that we'd done everything marvellously, but I think she must have put in some hard work on the kitchen for it had lost its tornadoish appearance and was now its usual, reasonably tidy, self.

Mum's good mood lasted and when after lunch Penny and Andrew asked if they could go to Charlbury with Cathy and me, she said yes without any argument at all. Rory, who tried about ten minutes later, got a very firm no. But, knowing Rory, none of us took that as final. We left him pestering Mum and made a dash to the stable; we'd decided that as it was pouring with rain we'd devote the afternoon to tack cleaning and we took everything into the Old Kitchen, turned up the oil heater, borrowed an electric fire from the dining-room and prepared to work in comfort, except for Penny, who'd decided that Harlequin's tack needed cleaning too and set off for the Old Rectory in a downpour, and Rory who could be heard still pestering.

We didn't hurry to start, but crouched around the electric fire discussing our trip to Charlbury until Penny came back, dripping wet and with Nick in tow.

"I found him wandering about the road," she said rather as though Nick were a stray dog, "and I thought he might as well come and do some work."

"Great," I said, "that means two people to each set of tack." I yelled up the passage for Rory to stop bullying Mum and come and help me, because Andrew was already dismantling Jess's bridle and as Penny had collected Nick I thought she'd better have him as her assistant.

We took things easily and talked and ate Nick's sweets – he still had some left – as we worked and we'd just finished and reassembled everything including Jess's bridle which Andrew had got into the most wonderful tangle, when Mum's voice called for tea-layers. Rory and Andrew said that they would go and by Rory's defiant back I guessed that Mum was in for it again. We asked Nick to stay to tea, but he seemed positively alarmed at the idea, and retreated through the side door hastily into the yard, saying that he simply must get home, he was expected.

SEVEN

We rose early on Monday morning and hurried through our jobs. Cathy and I walked up to the Firs to feed the ponies, because the parents aren't keen on the younger ones wandering about the roads in the dark; they did the home jobs.

When we got back Penny reported that the bantams had been very indignant at having to eat by the light of a hurricane lantern and had returned to bed, or rather perch, after a few mouthfuls. The ponies had raised no objections; they're only indignant when we're late.

Rory had so far failed to melt Mum's opposition, but at breakfast, which luckily we were having before Dad got back from his early morning rounds – we didn't want to draw his attention to the fact that we were going to Charlbury on the same day as Carmen – Rory suddenly burst into floods of tears and refused to be consoled by promises that he should unpack the Christmas decorations or make paper chains or mince pies. At the crucial moment, just as Mum's nerves reached breaking point, Cathy said, "Oh let him come; I'll look after him."

"After all, he is *eight*," added Penny, as though

that were the age of discretion.

Mum looked as though she might be weakening.

"Well, if he *is* coming," I said in deliberately dis-interested tones, "he'd better hurry up and change. The bus goes in half an hour." I had exaggerated a bit for there was the post office to visit on our way.

Mum gave in and while she was making Cathy promise "faithfully" not to let go of Rory's hand what-ever happened, he dashed upstairs to change into some-thing slightly more respectable than his worst jeans. When he reappeared, trousered and duffle-coated like the rest of us, we told Mum that we'd eat sandwiches and chocolate at the bus café and come home on the one-thirty bus or, if we missed it, the four-thirty, and then we rushed out of the house, with instructions to be careful and not to let Rory or Andrew get run over following us down the lane.

Mrs. Dent had our money ready and we signed Douglas Charles, Catherine Mary, Penelope Jane, Andrew John and Rory Ricardo Conway as rapidly as we could. Cathy said that I was to carry all of it and when I protested the others supported her. They said that (a) I was the eldest, (b) I had a wallet, (c) I had an inside pocket to my coat, so with a small groan at so much responsibility, I took the money and then we dashed out to wait for the bus which was now due.

It was late, but not much, and luckily there were very few passengers and the front seats were empty so Penny and Rory, who are inclined to feel sick, were able to sit behind the driver, which seems to be the least sick-making spot. Cathy and I sat behind them and Andrew sat next to the door and assisted the ancient passengers and the mothers with push chairs in and out.

It was a long, but interesting drive to Charlbury. Instead of staying on the main road as one does if one goes by car with one's parents, the bus wanders round the remote villages to either side of the road. On one side they stand amid the watery hedge-bound flatness of the vale and on the other, where narrow lanes climb and fall steeply, you come upon villages suddenly; farmhouses and thatched cottages, tight-packed in the clefts and hollows, and above them the bare line of the downs.

We amused ourselves by looking out and drawing each other's attention to horses, donkeys, Jersey herds and particularly nice houses, until at last we saw the steel grey of Charlbury cathedral's spire cutting the lighter grey of the winter sky.

"We're there," cried Rory excitedly. But of course we weren't, it took ages to get through the narrow streets and as the bus waited in queues at traffic lights, I began to have cold feet about the whole business.

The irresponsibility of allowing one's younger brothers and sisters to deceive the parents and take their money out of the post office to buy a cow grew more and more obvious. If only someone would buy Carmen for a hundred and fifty pounds, I thought, then we could visit the shops, find our parents some extra Christmas present, go home on the one thirty bus and forget the whole thing. Or would we, I wondered? Perhaps we'd be haunted for ever by visions of a poor old cow limping to the slaughterhouse after all those years of service to Charnworth.

And if we do buy her, I thought. And instantly a whole host of complications loomed up. We'd got to get her home to the Firs, we'd got to milk her night and morning, feed her, keep her secret until Cathy's good country home materialised; go on and on and on telling elaborate lies to our parents.

I was just going to suggest to Cathy that we called the whole thing off when she dug me in the ribs and said, "We're there."

We emerged into the bustle of the bus terminus and, not being sure of the way to the market, asked our driver. Then we set off, as directed, down a very seedy street and turning left at the bottom found ourselves in Abattoir Road. We turned in horror to gaze on the street sign. "What does it mean?" asked Rory. "It's French," said Cathy evasively. But Penny didn't mince matters. "Slaughterhouse, of course," she told him.

"Oh, I do hope we've got enough money," said Andrew anxiously. And my doubts began to leave me. It couldn't, I thought, be all that irresponsible to save cows from slaughter when whole societies existed to save horses. Jersey cows aren't like beef cattle, they're more intelligent and Carmen was an old and faithful friend. I felt for my wallet; it was still there and comfortingly fat. "Well, if we can't afford her, we can't," I told Andrew, "but at least we shall have done our best, and if she goes for more than a hundred pounds, it may be to someone who realises the value of her breeding and thinks she'll be good for a calf or two yet. We must try and see who's bidding for her, because we don't want to bid *against* a good country home."

From Abattoir Road a side entrance led into the market and we found ourselves in a huge covered building; on one side of us were auctioneers' offices and a café and on the other acres and acres of concrete and tubular steel pens. The auctioneers' office had a notice saying that catalogues were available so we availed ourselves of one and then went on past some pens where young calves of no particular breed waited for buyers. Andrew and Rory stopped and gazed miserably. "They'll be bought in a minute," I said, "and reared for beef, but there's no need to feel sorry for them, they'll have four lovely summers stuffing in water meadows before they're eaten." I was hoping that we wouldn't see any Jersey bull calves on their way to becoming dogs' meat; Carmen was going to be quite enough to take home. We looked into the main hall of the market where a horse sale was just about to begin and then we found our way to the ring where the Jersey sale was to take place. In all the pens around us now were smart little golden cattle. The cows were matronly with huge udders, the heifers pretty and agile, more like deer. There were solid-looking bulls with powerful chests and shoulders and muscles rippling under golden coats, lively young bulls, older bulls with angry eyes and sinister-looking bulls with very black faces. And everywhere there were white-coated herdsmen, leaning on pens or giving their charges a last polish.

"Carmen's in quite good company," I observed.

Suddenly Cathy, who'd been reading the catalogue, said, "They've got Charnworth Chieftain down here. Look!"

He was there all right. "The property of D. F. Smithson Esq.," the catalogue read and there was the date on which Chieftain was calved and the details of his pedigree and the prizes which he and his relations had won.

We all stood looking at each other in horror.

"The point is, who's come in with him?" I said. You

don't send a valuable bull to a sale alone. Usually Dad or Bill Martin comes as well as one of the other men.

"Oh Lord, I hope it's not Dad." Andrew sounded apprehensive.

"I shouldn't think so. Mum would have suggested that he gave us a lift," observed Cathy.

"Unless she thought Dad would be too gloomy about Carmen to want to be bothered by us," I pointed out.

"But why are they selling Chieftain?" asked Rory in miserable tones.

"Well, you have to sell some of your bulls," I told him. "Otherwise your herd becomes inbred. After all, they've got Cardinal and Crusader and then there's supposed to be a terribly good young one, isn't there? Isn't he the best they've ever bred?"

"Yes," Penny answered. "Dad wanted to call him Charnworth Crusoe, but Bill Martin said it wasn't a grand enough name for a future Supreme Champion, so he's called Churchill."

"It's quite different from selling Carmen," I told Rory, who still looked miserable. "Chieftain's young and valuable, he'll go to some posh herd and have dozens of glamorous wives. He's probably glad to get away from all his relations."

"I've found Carmen," said Cathy who was still reading the catalogue. "She's at the end under Late Entries and Miscellaneous."

We all looked at Carmen's brief particulars and the damning fact of her age, and then we tried to decide what to do. "We'd better find Chieftain and Carmen and see who *is* with them," suggested Penny.

"Wait a sec," I said as a rush of people to the ring told us that the sale had begun. "There'll only be one person looking after him now and with any luck it won't be Dad or Bill Martin; if they're here, they'll be studying prices at the ringside. "

"Chieftain is number fourteen," announced Cathy.

"Well, for goodness' sake let's go and find them," said Penny, who was tired of standing about.

"Not all of us," I objected, "it's too obvious."

Cathy said she'd stay with Andrew and Rory so Penny and I set off in search of the Charnworth contingent. We found them quite easily and George White – one of the under cowmen – seemed to be in charge. We decided to be bold and, making out that we were on a shopping expedition and had just come into the sale for a look, asked him if Dad or Mr. Martin were there.

"No," he answered, "'tis only me. Your Dad's got his hands full with Mr. Smithson and Bill wouldn't come on account of Carmen being sold."

"Are you staying to lead her in?" I asked as the awful thought struck me.

"No," he shook his head. "If Chieftain fetches his reserve I'm going straight back with the driver, 'e's waiting till then. I've arranged with one of the lads to take Carmen in. She won't fetch that much. She's ricked that leg of 'ers in the truck and she can 'ardly 'obble, poor old cow. There's no reserve on 'er; she's going for what she'll fetch."

We all looked at Carmen and sighed. Then Penny and I agreed, rather falsely, that we must get back to our shopping, we said good-bye and went to find the others.

"It all seems to be working out quite well," observed Cathy, when we told them what George White had said.

"Except that Carmen doesn't come in for absolutely

hours," grumbled Penny.

"Yes, I'm afraid we've had the half past one bus," I agreed gloomily, wondering what reason we could give to Mum for missing it.

"Let's go and look at the sale," suggested Rory. "It's jolly boring here."

The bidding was brisk and the prices seemed enormous to us. "We're never going to be able to afford Carmen," said Cathy.

"There are all up and coming," I reminded her. "Carmen's a has-been. Anyway, you don't go for dogs' meat at this sort of price."

We watched cow after cow sold and it became unbearably stuffy in the crowd round the sale ring. Soon Rory began to complain that he couldn't see.

"Only two more before Chieftain," Cathy told him. Then Andrew announced that he was feeling "funny" and he certainly looked green; we hastily removed him from the crowd and sat him down on a convenient bale of straw. We didn't see Chieftain sold, but we heard the bidding go up and up until he was knocked down for fourteen hundred pounds.

"Lord," said Andrew, reviving now that he was out of the crush, "the F.W. will be richer than ever."

"It'll go in tax," I told him.

Penny was fidgeting again. "What on earth are we going to do now?" she demanded. "We can't just wait here for hours and hours."

It was Cathy who suggested a visit to the horse sale and we set off with Rory and Penny in the lead and me toiling behind trying to calculate how long it would take for the auctioneer to get to Carmen if he was selling a cow every six minutes. It worked out about half past one.

The horse sale was rather depressing. The horses were mostly old with hollow backs or else they had things wrong with them. We decided that we'd never seen so many capped hocks, big knees, windgalls and bowed tendons under one roof. The ponies weren't so dilapidated, but a lot of them were Harlequin's type, cobby with large heads and small eyes, and they all looked either dejected or anxious. When we'd inspected all the horses and ponies, both the sold and the still to be sold, we had a look at the saddlery and then decided to go and keep Carmen company. The sight of doughnuts in the market café window reminded us that it was nearly lunch-time and we stopped to count our money. We couldn't spend any of the post office money until Carmen's fate was decided but we made a collection of everything else. We all seemed broke, me especially for I had already borrowed next week's pocket money from Mum to pay Andrew back and for my bus fare.

We managed to raise just enough money for five doughnuts, I think there was a couple of pence over, and then, munching hungrily we went to see Carmen. She seemed very perturbed by her situation, she was straining at her halter rope and mooing indignantly, but she didn't seem to find any consolation in our pats and soothing words. Chieftain was still in a near-by pen, but he was being watched over by a stranger so we decided that George White had gone. As the moment of buying Carmen drew nearer, I began to have cold feet again. Rory was getting bored and tormenting Andrew by putting bits of straw down his neck; Penny was fidgeting, and seeing that the crowd round the sale ring had thinned I suggested that we went back to watch.

The best animals had evidently been sold, for the ones

that remained were fetching much lower prices, I studied the methods of bidding. Some people seemed to manage with a twitch of an eyebrow or a nod of the head, but they were old hands, I decided. When it came to Carmen I was going to make sure that I was noticed and a firm wave of the catalogue seemed to be the recognised method. I had taken out my wallet and was counting the notes to make absolutely sure we had one hundred and fifteen pounds, when a tremendous commotion broke out in the yard outside where the cattle trucks load and unload. There were shouts and yells and a tremendous crash and more shouting – it sounded as though something terrific was happening. "Here, hold this a sec," I said to Cathy, handing her the catalogue and wallet, "I'm just going to see." I sprinted through a crowd of people all rushing for the main door and met another crowd in retreat. "Look out," they cried, "there's a bull got away."

I wanted to see for myself so I pressed on and emerged to see a Jersey bull out on the tarmac between the sheep pens and the cattle trucks. He was looking round him belligerently and a circle of men armed with sticks and pitchforks advanced slowly. Suddenly I realised that it was Charnworth Chieftain. . .

EIGHT

I hurried to join Chieftain's would-be capturers. "He's all right," I told them. "He's really quiet. Honestly."

"Ah, they're all quiet until they put someone in hospital," said an elderly farmer beside me. "They tried to hurry this one and he didn't like it. The chap who was leading him into the lorry, his bullstaff broke and the bull fell back over the side of the ramp. Now he's had enough. Let him quieten down," he called to the pitchfork brigade.

Everyone seemed to be giving advice. "Drive 'im into a sheep pen"; "Get him into a corner and back the lorry up to him." "Wait a minute." "Hurry up before 'e has time to get any ideas in 'is head."

"Can't we just catch him?" I suggested, wishing that George White were still here to cope. But at that moment Chieftain lowered his head and gave a terrible roaring bellow. He pawed the ground angrily, bellowed again and then charged. The circle of men held steady for a moment, then it wavered and, as Chieftain came on relentlessly, broke. "Shut the gates," yelled someone. But it was too late, Chieftain had also seen the open gates leading into Station Road and, his charge slowing to a rapid trot, he went through. With the pitchfork and stick brigade I ran in pursuit.

Unfortunately Chieftain hadn't turned towards the station where we might have cornered him in the car park; he'd turned right-handed and was trotting quickly in the direction of the town.

Station Road was practically empty, one or two passers-by waved their arms and shouted "Shoo", but when Chieftain lowered his head and bellowed threateningly they took refuge in the nearest doorway and let him go on. No one seemed to have a plan. We just ran after Chieftain breathlessly, hoping that some method of capture would present itself. One cattle-truck driver stopped at the first telephone kiosk saying that he'd ring the police and the rest of us ran on. Station Road comes out in Victoria Place and a choice of four roads presented itself. Chieftain kept straight on and took Church Street, which brought a loud groan from the pursuers. "Straight down into the town," said someone. Then they began to shout, trying to attract the attention of people farther down the street. "Turn 'im back, mate," they were calling, and "Don't let 'im get down in the town." But it was easier said than done, I thought, and the passers-by seemed to agree. Most of them were sheltering in doorways, behind trees or parked cars; they peered out with horrified faces as we swept by. Only one brave old lady stepped off the pavement and out into the road. "Shoo, shoo," she cried in a high, cracked voice and she waved her shopping bag and umbrella, but the crowd behind Chieftain was much more formidable than the one old lady ahead, lowering his head he gave a menacing bellow and increased his speed. The old lady stuck it to the very last moment and by then the crowd around me were shouting at her to get out of the way. She tried to, stumbled and fell. Chieftain slowed up and eyed her small, brittle-looking body, wondering whether to gore and crush his enemy. I longed for a pitchfork in my hands and we all ran faster, shouting. Chieftain trotted on. About six people stopped to pick up the old lady who lay with a sad mess of smashed eggs and spilt shopping in the road; the rest of us ran on. Some of the older and portlier farmers and truck drivers were getting left behind. There were new faces beside me, less countrified ones and I noticed with foreboding that we were nearly all unarmed. Church Street descended steeply and below I could see the Broadway, Charlbury's chief shopping street; the road was jammed with cars and buses, the pavements crammed with people Christmas shopping. It would be murder, I thought, if Chieftain got down there. I looked around desperately, seeking some way of stopping him, but short of a road block it seemed that nothing would. I looked down again at the people shopping quite unaware of the danger drawing near. I felt myself growing cold with fear as I thought of the carnage Chieftain would cause in that crammed street.

Ahead was a cross-roads where the narrowed end of the Broadway came up to join Church Street and without hesitation Chieftain trotted on, but coming up the rise out of the Broadway was a huge furniture van. The driver caught sight of Chieftain and acted quickly. He zigzagged his enormous van about the road while his mate leaned over and pressed a hand upon the horn. Chieftain stopped and gazed in horror. We in the front of the pursuing crowd stopped too and threw all our weight into holding those behind us; we had to keep the cross-roads clear at all costs. Chieftain turned back; he looked at the noisy horde bursting out of Church Street and turned hastily into the dignified quiet of High Street. Waving gratefully at the furniture van, we turned right-handed in pursuit. One of the few truck drivers left came alongside me. "They're driving him too fast now," he said breathlessly. "He's getting tired,. but with this lot behind he hasn't a chance to quieten down. Let's see if we can slow them up a bit."

"Steady there," and "Not so fast," we shouted at the crowd as we slowed down ourselves. But the yelling horde behind pressed on and engulfed us; we had to run if we were to stay in the front. It was then that Andrew and Rory caught up with me. Their faces were scarlet with running and excitement. "Oh Lord," I groaned. "You shouldn't have come. For goodness' sake stay with Andrew, Rory. Don't get lost whatever you do." He nodded. He evidently hadn't much breath left. But I knew he could keep up with Andrew; he's a very good runner for his age. As for me I was grateful, for the first time in my life, for the cross-country runs we are made to take at school. I had got my second wind and I felt good for several miles yet. I put on a spurt, threaded my way through the hurrying crowd and got back in the lead. Chieftain was trotting rapidly along High Street. Between sober bookshops, high-class antique businesses, societies for the propagation of religious literature, hat shops with windows full of sedate and purple hats for bishops' wives and oak-beamed tea shops offering cream teas. People rushed to their windows and doors. Black-coated clerics stared in amazement and someone shouted that there was a park at the top of the street.

The cattle-truck driver, who'd reappeared, and I

looked at each other with relief. It seemed that the end
was in sight. On our left the cathedral spire soared into
the sky. Ahead was a stone archway leading into a
narrow walled road. Beyond I could see ancient stone
buildings. We were coming into the precincts by the
back way, I thought happily. There would be gates and
no crowds. Perhaps we could shut Chieftain in some
archdeacon's garden until he'd calmed down. Relief
flowed over me as he trotted under the stone arch but, at
the same moment a door in the wall opened and out into
the road ahead of Chieftain poured a crowd of choirboys. They were laughing and shouting cheerfully.
When they saw Chieftain their shouts were of horror
but he had already turned; he came back through the
archway with lowered head and gave a blood-curdling
bellow as he looked at us.

He's going to charge, I thought, looking round for
Andrew and Rory. I couldn't see them and I couldn't
stop for the weight of the crowd behind. We leaders
advanced in an unwilling but unwavering line and
suddenly Chieftain lost his nerve. He fled from us and
the choirboys and plunged down a narrow alleyway.
Surging left-handed we followed. Monk's Passage read
the street sign above my head. The way was steep and
cobbled. Houses rose, tall and tightly packed, all round
us.

"Goes straight down to the Broadway, come out by
Marks and Spencers," shouted the cattle-truck driver in
a desperate voice.

I felt desperate too. We couldn't even stop to think
with this crowd behind us. Ahead I could see a youth
with a punk hair style pushing his bicycle up the passage.
When he saw Chieftain he stopped and put his bicycle

across the passage and standing behind it he began to shout and wave his arms. Chieftain was tired now, I think he would like to have stopped, but the choirboys had joined our crowd and as we in front tried to stop they squeezed by us and ran shrieking into the lead. Chieftain lowered his head, gave a despairing bellow and charged the bicycle. The punk jumped away at the last moment, tripped over a step and fell, cracking his head on the wall. Luckily Chieftain was venting his anger on the bicycle. There was a snapping of spokes, a scrunching of metal as he kneeled on it, then horning it out of his way he went on. Some people were helping the battered and bloody punk into their house. The rest of us surged on. The cattle-truck driver was swearing at the choirboys. Andrew and Rory were beside me again, they looked less excited and more anxious now that they'd seen what happened to people who got in Chieftain's way. Monk's Passage widened. We passed a back way into Marks and Spencers. If only, I thought, someone had had the sense to back a cattle truck into the alley and let down the ramp, but no one had. Unchecked Chieftain emerged into the Broadway with its jostling crowds and Christmas-decorated shops. He was greeted with screams. Horrible, nerve-rending screams, which rose and multiplied as the crowd panicked. Chieftain stood for a moment looking this way and that, then he gave a great roaring angry cry, turned right and charged the fleeing crowd, trying to clear a way for himself along the pavement. The screams were appalling. People dropped their shopping and ran. Motorists jammed on their brakes and pedestrians fled into the road, prams were abandoned, small children knocked down and the doorway of every shop was jammed with people fighting to get inside. Chieftain had cleared the pavement; he trotted along it, swinging his head from side to side daring anyone else to get in his way.

Suddenly the Broadway was full of policemen. Constables in helmets, high-ups in caps, police in patrol cars and on motor-bikes. They were directing the traffic up side streets, shooing people towards the less populated shops, picking up toddlers, collecting the prams. Gradually a plan emerged. Around Chieftain in the middle of the Broadway a great space had been cleared; ahead the cars were parked across the street in a solid block and behind the same thing had happened. He was penned in a great empty square except that across the Broadway from us the opening to Ship Street was unguarded. The cattle-truck driver was shouting at the choirboys to be quiet and stand still and other voices took up the cry, gradually order was restored. Chieftain, finding himself unpursued stood in the middle of his square with lowered head and heaving sides. The police were borrowing umbrellas from the crowds, one for each policeman. I wondered why. The cattle-truck driver gave me his pitchfork and produced a piece of cord from his pocket. "I'll just go and see if he'll let me catch him," he said. "I believe he's quiet enough in the ordinary way. You be ready with this fork though, if he goes for me."

"O.K.," I answered, feeling far from confident. But as the driver approached, talking soothingly, Chieftain eyed him with hate. He pawed the ground, lowered his head and gave a menacing bellow. The truck driver came back. "He won't have it," he said.

A police car's loud-speaker crackled into life. "We are now going to drive the animal up Ship Street," it announced. "An army unit is waiting at the top with rifles. Will everyone keep quiet please."

"Cor, they're going to shoot him then," said the driver. "That'll be fourteen hundred pounds gone west. He'd be all right if they could drive him somewhere and leave him to calm down." Behind me I heard Rory sniff.

The police were ready now; they had arranged themselves in a huge three-quarter circle with the open quarter on the entrance to Ship Street. They advanced on Chieftain slowly, gradually making the circle smaller and as they advanced each policeman opened and shut his umbrella, which he held in front of him like a shield, in a steady rhythmic motion. It was a nerve-racking sight.

Chieftain looked round at them, pawed the ground and gave a great bellow. Then he saw the entrance into Ship Street.

"Stand still," said the loud-speaker. And the blue circle stopped with all the umbrellas opened. Chieftain looked at the inviting entrance. He began to walk towards it. The crowd gave a great sigh of relief. I looked at his back sadly, he seemed, I thought, like some historic figure going uncomplainingly to his execution. It was a pity things had to end like this. Then without warning the silence was broken, there was the sudden roar of an engine and from out of one of the Ship Street yards swung a motor-bike. Unsuspectingly the rider swept down towards the Broadway. Chieftain turned and then with an enraged bellow he charged. He charged across the Broadway and straight at the line of police in front of us. They stood their ground; the one who bore the brunt of the charge actually impaled his umbrella on Chieftain's horns before he jumped to safety. Maddened, and partly blinded by the umbrella, Chieftain gave another great roar and charged on. We scattered with the rest of the crowd and watched with horror as Chieftain held to his course. With a tremendous crash he went straight through a shop window and disappeared from view. There were more crashes and screams from inside the shop. We ran forward to the window. The hole was surprisingly small but surrounded by great cracks and murderous-looking edges. Without a moment's hesitation Rory climbed through. Andrew followed him and cursing younger brothers I squeezes through after them. It was a dress shop, smart, but not terribly big. The window was full of tumbled models and splinters of glass and the door of the shop was jammed with people fighting to get out.

Chieftain stood by a counter, he had his back to us. His head was hanging and he looked broken, beaten and exhausted.

"Whoa, boy," we said. I looked at Rory and Andrew. "We can't all catch him and I'm the eldest," I said.

Their faces fell, but they stayed where they were and let me go up to Chieftain alone. He was far too tired to object. I talked to him and scratched his neck and then very gently I pulled the remnants of the umbrella off his horns. He was cut in several places and dripping blood on the fawn-carpeted floow, but the cuts were nothing to what you'd expect on a bull who's just charged a plate-glass window. "Can you see anything that would make a bull-staff?" I asked my brothers. There were plenty of jazzy-looking belts arrayed on a stand, but one can't control a full-grown bull in a proper head collar much less a flimsy affair made of belts.

"What sort of thing do you want?" asked a voice. And from behind the counter where she had evidently been taking cover appeared a very glamorous blonde.

"A piece of wood, short and stumpy; something like a cricket stump," I answered.

The blonde thought. "A shortie umbrella," she said, and disappeared into another department. The police had all gathered round the broken window and they looked as if they were regretting their regulation size, but they had the sense not to start breaking glass or making any more noise that would upset Chieftain. The shop doorway was still blocked by the people struggling to go out.

The blonde reappeared and handed me a short, fat umbrella in a scarlet sheath. "Will this do?" she asked. "It's our most expensive line, so it ought to be strong." "Thanks," I said. The handle was straight without hook or crook and had a thick scarlet cord threaded through it. "Any scissors?" I asked. "I'll have to cut this loop and tie it to the ring in his nose."

The blonde produced scissors and Chieftain made no objection to having an umbrella knotted to his ring by a scarlet cord. He seemed to have no fight left in him, but I didn't feel inclined to take risks. "Have you any rope or strong cord?" I asked the blonde. "Just in case the umbrella breaks." She hurried away. I called to Andrew. "Tell the police I've got him, more or less, and ask to have a cattle truck backed up to the shop door. We don't want the crowd frightening him again."

They'd cleared the shop doorway now and just as the blonde came back with a splendid piece of rope the police ushered in a couple of military types, armed to the teeth. They strode towards Chieftain. One of them, a sergeant, joined the blonde behind the counter, the other, a major with a stupid face and an exotic moustache, came up to me.

"Stand aside," he said, "I'm going to shoot the brute," and he produced a revolver.

NINE

"There's no earthly point in shooting him now we've caught him," I argued. "Besides, the police have sent for a cattle truck."

"The brute's mad," said the Major. "Been terrorizing the town all morning. Once a killer always a killer; like a dog that's tasted blood. Can't trust the brutes again."

"He hasn't killed anyone," I pointed out, "and someone has just paid fourteen hundred pounds for him. The new owner's not going to be particularly delighted to find you've shot him."

The Major looked peeved. "We were called out by the police to shoot a mad bull and I'm going to shoot it," he said obstinately, "and I'll thank you to get out of the way." I stayed where I was, or rather I moved a little nearer what I thought was the vulnerable spot on Chieftain's forehead. "Andrew," I called, "ask the police to send someone in here, a high-up if poss. And tell them to hurry up with that cattle truck."

The Major's face had darkened to a dusky red. I think he would have enjoyed shooting me as well as Chieftain. The blonde came to the rescue.

"I suppose you're an expert shot, Major?" she said with a dazzling smile. "I mean, they wouldn't call you out on a dangerous job like this if you weren't, would they? I expect you go big-game hunting and all that." I thought she was rather overdoing the glad-eye business, but the Major seemed to fall for it.

"Fair to mod," he answered, brushing up the ends of the exotic moustache. "Get a stag occasionally and a bit of rough shooting most week-ends."

There was activity then among the police round the shop door and I hoped for a cattle truck or at least some-one to remove the Major, but a jaunty figure in cavalry twill trousers and a hacking jacket was ushered in.

"I'm a veterinary surgeon," he announced as he bustled up. "They've sent me to put this chap down. Run amok, I hear. Nice-looking bull too. Great pity, very bad luck. Whoa, boy, whoa," he went on ap-proaching Chieftain nervously and suddenly producing a humane killer from behind his back.

"Look here," said the Major, "they sent for me to shoot the brute and I got here first and I intend to do it."

"What's holding you up then?" asked the vet. "Waiting for ammunition?" He laughed loudly and then looked at Chieftain apprehensively, but the bull was much too tired to object.

"Nothing of the sort," answered the Major angrily, "it's entirely . . ."

"Well, now I'm here I'll do the deed," interrupted the vet; "the public prefer to hear that an animal has been put down with a humane killer. So if you don't mind . . . Stand a bit more to the left, old chap," he said to me.

"But I do mind; I object most strongly," stormed the

Major. "I was called from my luncheon to shoot this animal and I got here first. I have the prior claim."

"Jolly bad luck and all that," said the vet, "but you should have got on with it. Turn his head a bit more to the right, old chap," he told me.

I turned Chieftain's head firmly to the left and moved myself to the right. With any luck, I thought, the Major will shoot the vet. But I was very glad when Andrew and Rory appeared. "The police seem in a bit of a muddle," Andrew announced. "First of all they wanted to shoot Chieftain but when they heard how much he was worth some of them went off to telephone his owner. That'll probably take ages. But the nice driver has gone to fetch his cattle truck and he won't be long now."

"There," I told the vet and the Major. "The police are contacting the owner, we'll have to wait."

The blonde spoke quickly. "If you gentlemen would like to come through to the staff canteen you could have a cup of coffee while you're waiting. I'm sure you must need it," she said, managing to give two glad eyes at once.

"Not a bad idea," answered the Major returning the glad eye.

"An excellent idea," said the vet giving the Major a dirty look.

"Come along, Sergeant," called the Major and as she marched her party off the blonde turned and gave me a wink.

Andrew said, "Oh good, here it is at last," and I looked round to see our friend the truck driver and a white-coated herdsman come into the shop. The herdsman, who evidently worked for Chieftain's new owner, seemed very depressed. All the time we were untying the shortie umbrella and exchanging it for the proper bullstaff he'd brought, he lamented. "Cor, you 'ave led us a dance. Terrible damage all round the town, fifteen people taken to 'ospital. I don't know what the boss is going to say." Then he looked Chieftain over. "Cut to pieces," he murmured sadly, "fourteen hundred quid and 'e's cut to pieces before we get 'im 'ome. I don't know what the boss is going to say."

"All's well that ends well," said our friend the truck driver cheerfully. "Come on, mate, let's get 'im out of 'ere. They say the Manager's back from his lunch and raising merry hell outside. Accused Superintendent George of deliberately driving the bull into his shop."

"And the Major and the vet will have finished their coffee in a minute," I added, "and they'll be back wanting to shoot him."

"Shoot 'im! Whatever would the boss say?" moaned Chieftain's herdsman. "Oh dear, look at that carpet, all them bloodstains. Whatever's the boss going to say if he isn't insured?"

We turned Chieftain and his lamenting herdsman and propelled them both towards the shop door. Chieftain looked as docile as an old sheep and he moved stiffly, evidently his cuts and bruises had stiffened up as he stood in the shop. The cattle truck had been backed up to the door, the ramp lay over the pavement and policemen held the slatted side gates firmly in position. The precautions looked very unnecessary as the weary Chieftain dragged himself up the ramp; but few people trusted him; there were a hundred hands eager to close ths side gates and slam the ramp shut on the mad bull.

I sighed with relief and was just becoming aware that

my legs ached and that I was madly hungry, when I saw
Cathy running towards us.

"Oh Rory, you are a *beast*," she said, "I've been
looking for you everywhere. I thought you'd probably
been trampled to death or something. You are mean
going off like this when you know I promised Mum I
wouldn't let go of you all day."

"Well, I stayed with Andrew and Douglas," Rory
defended himself. "You knew I'd gone with . . ."

"But Cathy, what about Carmen?" I interrupted,
realising with sudden horror that in all the excitement
I'd forgotten the poor old cow.

"Penny's there," answered Cathy, still indignant.
"When I found that Rory had gone I gave her the
money; she said that she didn't mind bidding."

"Oh Lord! Well, come on; we'd better see what's
happening. Does anyone know the way? I'm lost."

"Yes, I know the way," answered Cathy. "I've been
walking round and round this beastly city looking for
Rory."

It seemed miles to the market. We were all feeling
worried about Carmen and cross with ourselves or each
other and terribly weary. Cathy and I practically
dragged Rory along, for now the excitement was over
he was tired and tearful. Andrew didn't help matters
either for every few moments he said, "Oh, I *do* hope
Penny got her," or "Do you *think* Penny got her?" or,
"Supposing Penny didn't know how to bid?" making
me feel more and more guilty at having forsaken Carmen
for the excitement of the chase.

When we reached the main gate of the market we
saw Penny waiting for us. "What on earth have you all
been doing?" she asked. "It's absolutely ages since I

bought Carmen; she's in the cattle truck waiting to go and the driver's getting impatient."

"You got her?" asked Andrew dancing round. "Oh, well done, Penny. Good old Penny," he exclaimed, patting her on the back.

"How much did she cost?" asked Rory.

"Only twenty-five pounds," answered Penny. "There weren't many people there; everyone had rushed off like you, to chase that bull, and she was limping terribly. But," she looked at me defiantly, "I spent the rest of the money; I've bought a horse."

Andrew and Rory gave shrieks of joy. Cathy and I stood gaping at her in open-mouthed surprise.

"You haven't?" I said. "You haven't done anything so absolutely idiotic?"

"Yes, I have," Penny answered calmly.

"What sort of horse?" asked Andrew.

"A thoroughbred," Penny answered proudly. "A bay mare bred in Ireland; she's fifteen one, just the right size for Douglas, but she's very thin."

"Well, you go and unbuy her then," I stormed angrily. "You're mad. How can we just take home a horse? You know what a muddle everything is in."

"She was a terrific bargain," said Penny. "I got her for a hundred pounds. Luckily Nick turned up and lent me the money for the cattle truck home. Now do come on, they're both loaded and the driver'll be getting livid."

"Penny, you can't . . ." I began. But she wasn't listening, she'd hurried off towards the cattle truck and was answering Andrew's and Rory's excited questions as calmly as if we bought a horse every day of our lives.

"She's crazy," I told Cathy. "She's absolutely

crackers. What does she think Dad will say when we roll up with a horse? And if we tell him about the horse, he'll find out about Carmen. The girl's mad."

"Well, if you'd stayed instead of going off after Chieftain," replied Cathy disagreeably, "everything would have been all right."

It was true, of course. I'd been mad to leave Penny alone in a market with a wallet of money. But then, I hadn't known that Cathy wasn't there exercising her restraining influence. Though actually, as I had to admit to myself, I hadn't thought about it at all; in the excitement of the chase I'd clean forgotten Carmen. I am irresponsible, I thought bitterly, and depression closed over me in great dark waves.

There were excited cries coming from the cattle truck when we reached it. A fat driver appeared·and asked rather wearily if we were the lot and when we said we were he pushed us in through a small trap-door, slammed it shut and a moment later we were off. I found myself with all the others in a small compartment. Separated from us by a partition stood a gaunt bay mare with dull eyes and a neck so thin it seemed unable to hold up her head. Beyond her was Carmen.

Cathy was looking at the mare with rather a horrified expression. "How old is she?" she asked.

"The man swore she was seven." Nick's voice spoke up from a dark corner.

"Oh, hullo," I said without enthusiasm. And, "They always say that; seven's their favourite age."

"I don't think she's terribly old; I looked at her teeth and they didn't seem all that long." Penny spoke with more diffidence now. "You look, Douglas."

I wouldn't look. I was much too angry about the

whole business. I didn't like the idea of telling Dad we'd bought a horse and I didn't like the idea of not telling him. It was going to be bad enough keeping Carmen secret; this was the last straw.

"If she isn't about thirty, she's got something pretty deadly wrong with her," I said. "Redworm to begin with and I should think they've perforated her intestine. And if you didn't get a warranty or a vet's certificate she's probably lame as well."

Penny began to sniff. "I only bought her because she seemed so sad and thin and I thought we'd fatten her up and you could ride her next holidays, because I know you'll say you're too big to ride Merlin any more," her voice trailed away miserably.

Cathy turned on me then. "You're beastly, Douglas," she said. "Anyone nice who had a hundred pounds would have bought her when they saw her looking so half-starved and miserable even if she is lame and sick and no use for riding."

I thought Cathy was being unfair; I felt that she ought to have some fellow feeling for me as she has to be the eldest in the term. Generally she is a very reasonable person, but by her mouth, tight shut in an obstinate line, and her blazing eyes I knew that reasoning was no use now. "All I can say is that I think Penny's mad to buy a horse of any sort while the parents are worried to death lest Dad loses his job," I told her. "I think we're mad to buy Carmen, but to saddle ourselves with a half-starved horse as well . . ."

"If the worst comes to the worst, we can find them both good homes," argued Cathy.

"But if Dad loses his job we'll have to leave Nutsford," said Andrew in a panic-stricken voice."

"He's not going to lose his job." Cathy spoke firmly. "Douglas is just being difficult."

After that I gave up. I saw down in a corner on some not frightfully clean straw and brooded drearily.

Cathy and Penny stared straight ahead of them with stormy expressions. Rory asked Andrew how high he thought the mare could jump. Silently Nick handed round chocolate – a whole bar each. As I ate I realised how hungry I was; it seemed centuries since we'd eaten the doughnuts. I looked at my watch and found that it was half past three.

"Oh Lord," I said. "What on earth are we going to tell Mum? Not only have we missed the one-thirty bus, but we're going to arrive before the four-thirty is due."

"Say you hitch-hiked," suggested Nick.

"It's not popular; she thinks the girls will get murdered."

"We could say we saw a cattle truck driver we knew and he said he was going through Charnworth and offered us a lift. At least the cattle truck part would be true," said Cathy.

"All right," I agreed wearily. "And why did we miss the bus?"

"Because we were helping to catch the bull, of course," said Penny. "We needn't mention the market, but you'd better tell us exactly what happened, because Cathy and I must have been somewhere near too, only we got parted from you in the crowd."

Andrew and Rory, both talking at once, related our adventures and I was still correcting their version of what the vet and the Major and the glamorous shop assistant had said, when the cattle truck stopped and the driver's voice called, "Is this the place? There's no name on the gate, but we're nearly in Charnworth and there's any amount of firs." We peered out through the ventilation slits and announced that it was.

We unloaded rapidly. The driver was in a hurry and we had no desire to linger in the road with our secret animals. Cathy took Carmen and I led the mare; Penny and Nick had to pay the driver. The mare was quiet enough. She followed me without a flicker of interest in her dull eyes; she obviously had no strength left to care whether her new home was good or bad. Jess and Merlin came trotting up, their ears pricked and their heads high, to investigate the visitors. Merlin spoke to the mare politely, nose to nose, but Jess squealed and stamped and humped pretence kicks in her direction in the most unwelcoming way.

I turned the mare loose, but Cathy led Carmen on to the shed. "Bags first milk," she called over her shoulder.

Rory, Andrew and I fetched hay, a whole bale instead of the usual half. Jess was still behaving badly; she chased the mare from pile to pile with villainous faces and angry squeals. We had to arrange dozens of small heaps,. but even then the mare barely had time for a mouthful, before Jess was after her again.

"Tomorrow," I said, looking at the thin, shambling figure through the damp dusk, "we'll bring her up an enormous bucket of feed," and then we went into the shed to see how Cathy's milking was going.

TEN

The questions we answered that evening when we reached home and the lies we told, were like something out of a nightmare.

To begin with, Mum was in a panic. She seemed to have spent her day imagining us falling under buses and losing Rory and when three o'clock came and we had failed to appear she had feared the worst. Dad had arrived home at half past four with the news of a bull amok in Charlbury and frantic telephone calls to the police station and hospital were only just averted by our appearance. We admitted to having been in the thick of it. I told the whole story truthfully, except for being vague about the point where we had joined the chase and allowing them to think that the girls were somewhere in the crowd and that I'd kept a tight hold on Rory. Dad thought it funny, especially the Major and the vet, and became more cheerful than he had been for ages. Mum was less amused; she thought we might easily have been tossed, gored or trampled to death. She said that she was never going to let us go to Charlbury on our own again.

Our method of getting home needed an absolute spate

of lies and then we were nearly sunk over the wretched present. In the excitement we'd forgotten all about it and when Mum asked if we'd got what we went in for we looked at her with vacant expressions. Then, suddenly realising, we all laughed loudly and said, "Yes, *rather*," in unnaturally hearty tones, but that at least was true.

Later in the evening, after we'd eaten an enormous tea, Dad had a telephone call from Chieftain's new owner, apparently put on to him by Mr. Smithson; he, the new owner, wanted to know whether Chieftain was dangerous and if he'd ever gone amok before. Dad calmed him down and then came through to the Old Kitchen to tell us about it. We were all busy, Cathy and I addressing envelopes for belated cards for our uncles and aunts, the others packing their presents in last year's Christmas paper and giving constant cries of "Secret", and "Don't look." It was hard to think of answers for Dad's, "I can't think why you didn't recognise him." Avoiding his mystified glance as much as possible, I answered vaguely. "He *did* have a familiar sort of look," I said, and, "I've never seen him roused before," and, "Of course Jersey bulls all look a bit alike."

We heaved a joint sigh of relief when Dad, still looking mystified, took himself off.

On Tuesday morning Penny wakened me to the usual sound of pouring rain and with the information that it was our turn to fetch the ponies and that she had bagged milk. "I bags stay in bed," I groaned unco-operatively. "And it's too early; it's still pitch dark," I objected retiring under the bed-clothes.

"Carmen'll be mooing the place down; she's used to being milked at six," said Penny jolting me into wakefulness. I groaned miserably as I remembered the happenings of the day before and all the hideous complications we'd had to face. "All right," I told her, climbing out of bed, "I won't be long."

I washed and dressed, looked enviously in on Andrew and Rory who were still senseless humps under their bedclothes, attired myself in boots and Dad's army surplus garment and joined Penny in the stable. She had collected two buckets and she stood looking at the corn bin with a perplexed expression. "How much of everything do cows eat?"

I scratched my sleepy head. "They don't eat whole oats," I said. "Oh, yes, you feed them according to their milk yields. Oh Lord, don't give her too many oats, we don't want gallons and gallons of milk; Cathy chucked away a whole bucketful last night; it's an awful waste."

"Yes, but *how* much?" asked Penny.

"Two scoops of oats and none of bran," I hazarded a guess. "And then we'll reduce the oats gradually until we find that good home. The mare can have a bucketful," I added, taking the bucket and filling it to the brim. Storm appeared wagging and grinning and we invited her to come with us; she declined politely, looking over her shoulder at the house and trying to explain that she was just waiting for Dad. We took the hint and sneaked past the kitchen window concealing our buckets as best we could. Then we walked in sleepy silence, through the driving rain. As we crossed the river the blackness of the sky lightened to a dismal grey and as we climbed Sutton's Hill we heard Carmen's voice demanding indignantly that she should be milked.

"Thank heavens the Gordon-Kellys are in South Africa," I observed. "If they were here they'd be on the telephone to Dad by now."

"Yes. 'Mr. Conway, I'm afraid I must ask you to be so kind as to remove this new cow; my wife simply cannot stand the noise,'" said Penny imitating Mr. Gordon-Kelly's pompous tones.

Carmen was waiting at the gate with Jess and Merlin, and Penny and I both looked round anxiously for the mare; she was huddled miserably in the lee of the spinney. We fetched halters, caught our new acquisitions and led them to the shed. The mare was shaking with cold and Carmen was limping badly; they were a depressing sight and Penny and I avoided each other's eyes. We managed to fit them both into the shed; it was rather a squash, and as Penny began milking I took an armful of hay to Jess and Merlin who had assumed hurt expressions at the sight of the newcomers breakfasting when they weren't. "You're going to have your feeds when you get home," I told them. And then I went back to the shelter of the shed.

"Her udder's absolutely bursting," Penny told me. "I'm sure Cathy can't have milked her right out last night."

"She may have been upset after her travels and not given it all," I answered looking at the mare. "I've never seen a horse so cold," I observed. "I'm going to rub her down." I rubbed and wisped with handfuls of hay in an attempt to get the mare's circulation going and Penny milked and milked. Presently Carmen finished her feed and then she began to fidget. She swished her wet tail, catching Penny across the face, then she cow-kicked; her leg landed in the bucket and milk poured all over the shed floor. "Oh, you are a disagreeable old cow," said Penny crossly.

"It's practically breakfast-time," I told her, as I looked at my watch.

"Well, I'm being as quick as I can," answered Penny crosser still, "but she will fidget and there's masses more to come." She milked and milked and the sound of the milk drumming on the sides of the bucket came in regular and constrained spurts. The mare had stopped shaking so I offered to have a go with Carmen. Penny handed over the bucket and the oil-drum milking stool gladly and I put my head against Carmen's warm flank and went to work on the two quarters which still bulged with milk. I milked and milked and I began to realise that there was a vast difference between stripping cows that had already been milked by electricity, which was what we did when we helped Bill Martin, and milking a cow from scratch. My hands started to ache and Carmen swished and got me in the eye with the mucky end of her tail. Then she kicked over the bucket twice in quick succession and finally she kicked me and the oil-drum milking stool and the bucket all in an undignified heap.

"Oh hell and damnation!" I swore finding myself soaked in about a gallon of best grade Channel Island milk.

"I'll have another go," said Penny collecting up the bucket and stool. I mopped milk and mud from my clothes and muck from my face. Then I looked at my watch.

"Lord! It's after nine, Penny. We must go; she'll have to do," I exclaimed. "Anyway with any luck she'll start to dry off if we don't strip her properly."

"She'll moo the place down, you mean," said Penny pessimistically. We hastily turned Carmen and the mare loose and caught up Jess and Merlin. We vaulted on their wet muddy backs and cantered across the field to the gate. "What on earth reason are we going to give for being so late?" I asked as we trotted along the road.

"Jess wouldn't be caught," said Penny. "She was in one of her moods."

It seemed rather mean to blame Jess, but just occasionally in wet weather she is difficult to catch, so at least it was a likely excuse. We trotted the whole way home, except for the steepest part of Sutton's Hill, which warmed us and the ponies and we flung feeds in their mangers before dashing into breakfast. Dad had been in and gone out again, but Mum wanted to know what had happened to us, though the others showed an unusual lack of interest and changed the subject ceaselessly; we blamed Jess between mouthfuls of breakfast.

After we'd washed up and struggled with our beds we all retired to the Old Kitchen. Kathy, Andrew and Rory were dying to know how our new animals were, but we couldn't give them a very good report. "The mare's too well-bred to sleep out; she was terribly cold. I'm sure she'll get pneumonia if we don't put her in at night." I said.

"Yes, she's awfully thin-skinned," agreed Penny. "And then there's Carmen's leg."

"Supposing we ride in the field this morning?" I suggested. "Then the non-riders could treat Carmen and clear a space in the shed for the mare to sleep in." They all agreed and Cathy said, "We must think of a name for her. 'The mare' sounds beastly."

Then, hearing hoofs outside in the lane, we all dashed to the window thinking that the ponies had escaped, but to our surprise we saw Nick riding in on Harlequin. He waved triumphantly when he caught sight of us. We all

ran out to the yard to meet him. He seemed frightfully
pleased at having caused such a sensation, though
Penny damped hom down by pointing out that
Harlequin's noseband was outside his cheek pieces and
his throat lash was too tight. But the rest of us told him
that he was really clever to catch Harlequin and nice to
save us a filthy wet walk.

It was raining less violently and after a long discussion
and many anxious glances at the sky we decided to ride,
and after more discussion we decided that Nick,
Andrew and Rory should ride, as the rest of us wanted to
see to Carmen and the mare. Leaving the others to
saddle up I ran upstairs and whipped a bottle of embrocation from the bathroom medicine cupboard, and then
walking and riding we set off for the Firs. As we went
we tried to think of a name for the mare. Cathy
favoured an Irish one and Nick supported her, but Rory
wanted to call her Sherry and Andrew had set his heart
on Romany, though he gave way when Penñy pointed
out that she wasn't a gipsy type at all, but a thoroughbred. The only Irish names I could think of were Biddy
and Molly and, as Penny said, they weren't grand
enough; Biddy was only suitable for cobs and ponies.
We tried to think of the names of horses in Somerville
and Ross's books but we could only remember the
Quaker and that didn't seem to suit our mare's character,
not that we knew much about it, but we felt that when
she was restored to health she was more likely to be a
light-hearted type than a Quaker. We tried to think of
the names of places in Ireland and we weren't particularly brilliant at that either; Kilkenny was the best and
then Nick suggested Colleen and someone else Folly. I
remembered that most of the horses in the Irish jumping

team had names which began with Bally and after that Rory was maddening and rode along yelling Bally Nick and Bally Pen and Bally everything else he could think of.

Penny began to regret that we couldn't consult Mum, who's good at names and then Cathy thought of Shamrock. It was Irish and it sounded nice. It didn't seem silly now she was a wreck, and yet it would still be all right if she turned into the handsome thoroughbred Penny expected. And it suited any character. We thought about it and gradually everyone agreed that it would do.

When we reached the Firs I suggested to Nick, Andrew and Rory that they should have a handy hunter competition, and we told them to beware of jumping high or galloping fast as the ground was slippery. They rode away planning to time-keep with Nick's very superior-looking watch and to include opening and shutting the spinney gate in the course, and we set to work.

"Carmen first?" asked Penny. "Yes," I agreed, "because when we've made the stable we'd better shut the shivering mare, I mean Shamrock, in it. She's just as wet as she was before breakfast; all that drying was wasted."

Penny and I held Carmen while Cathy gently rubbed on the embrocation and at first she behaved very well. Then it began to sting I suppose, for she hopped up and down on her three good legs kicking wildly with the fourth and then she charged round the shed, throwing us all against the wall. She was far worse than Chieftain. We hung on to the halter rope and eventually she calmed down, but not completely we had great difficulty in taking the halter off, every time we tried she threw her head about and our arms became entangled in her horns. When at last we managed to free her we agreed that we much preferred horses to cows. "She doesn't appreciate our efforts at all," I complained watching the indignant figure hobble away.

"No, it's bitter. She thinks we've deprived her of her smart milking parlour and her nice electric milking machine and her huge meals and white-coated attendants," said Cathy. "She doesn't realise that she was nearly dogs' meat."

"I know it's wrong to want gratitude, but it's a bit hard to be *so* disapproved of," I grumbled.

"Shamrock will appreciate us," said Penny. "She hasn't had a comfortable home with plenty to eat like Carmen. Let's ride her when we've made her stable; just a minute each wouldn't hurt her surely?"

ELEVEN

Cathy and I agreed that just a minute each couldn't possibly hurt Shamrock, in fact it would warm her up and the thought of trying out our new horse lent strength to our arms. We heaved hay bales with ease and piled them into a smaller but taller stack. Then we put hurdles between Shamrock and the hay, we didn't want her to pull the pile down on her head, and we used jump poles and string to make a sliprail front to the open shed. We bedded down the mud floor with a bale of musty hay and then Penny took a halter and went to fetch Shamrock in. The handy hunter was over and the horsemen came trotting across to ask what they should do next. "Lend us a saddle," I answered, "we can't possibly ride Shamrock bareback." We all looked at the razor edge of her spine.

"Which would fit best?" asked Andrew.

"I don't think any of them are going to fit," I answered, "but it's only for a minute."

"Merlin's is the narrowest," said Cathy, "and I should think the girth would go round her." Nick dismounted. "Merlin's nice bareback," I told him consolingly as I took the saddle away.

"Now you can have a trotting race," said Cathy.

"Bareback trotting, great," exclaimed Andrew and he and Rory dismounted and snatched off their saddles.

We borrowed Merlin's bridle, leaving poor Nick to make do with a halter. The bridle just fitted Shamrock in the last hole but the saddle didn't fit anywhere. However with Penny's scarlet scarf as a wither pad we didn't think riding on it for a few minutes would do any harm. Cathy and I said Penny could have first ride because she so obviously wanted it. We held Shamrock while she climbed into the saddle with cries of "She's terrifically tall, miles taller than Merlin," and we followed when she rode towards the end of the field where the bareback trotting race wasn't taking place. Shamrock looked awful. Her head hung drearily at the end of her stiff thin neck and her long hind legs trailed behind the rest of her. She looked as old as the hills, very thin and hopelessly dejected. Penny persuaded her into a shambling trot and circled round us, then she tried to canter. Shamrock trotted faster forging and stumbling, and then, as Penny urged her on she lurched into an unbalanced gallop. In a few moments Penny pulled up and rode back to us; there were tears in her eyes. "She's absolutely *awful* to ride," she told us miserably.

I didn't know what to say to that. "Let Douglas try her and see what he thinks," suggested Cathy. Penny dismounted and I climbed into the saddle. I'd seen Shamrock ridden and I knew more or less what to expect and my disappointment wasn't as acute as Penny's, but I didn't ride for long; the poor horse felt too tired and weak for it to be any pleasure. I handed her over to Cathy. "She'll be quite different when she's fat," I told Penny as we watched Cathy ride away.

"She's half-starved; she's bound to feel awful."

The bareback trotters joined us shrieking cheerfully, Nick had fallen off once, Andrew twice and Rory would have fallen off only Jess had stopped and put her head up at the crucial moment. Their cheerfulness vanished when they noticed Penny's face.

"What's the matter?" asked Andrew anxiously.

"Nothing," I answered. But Penny was determined to wallow in misery. "It's just that Shamrock's absolutely beastly to ride," she said fiercely. "She's stiff and stumbles all the time and you can hardly get her to canter."

"Oh, for heaven's sake, Penny," I protested as I saw two large tears run down her face. "You didn't expect to buy a perfectly-schooled show hack for a hundred pounds, did you? Anyway, look, she's going better for Cathy. It's partly because you're used to bouncy little ponies that you don't like her. She won't be too bad when she's fat."

"*If* she ever gets fat," said Penny bitterly.

Cathy rode up to us and patted Shamrock before dismounting. "I don't think she's ever been schooled; she doesn't seem to understand anything. But when she's fit and we've schooled her I don't see why she shouldn't be a nice ride." Cathy managed to sound optimistic, and I hastily supported her.

"She'll go like a bomb," I said with a conviction I didn't feel. "With those hind legs, she's bound to be fast," and then as the drizzle became a downpour once more, I added, "Oh hell! Let's take her in before she gets soaking wet again."

The riders saddled up and went off to have a walk, trot and canter race while the rest of us dried Shamrock and provided her with a bucket of water and a huge heap of hay. Then we stood in the shelter of the shed waiting for the race to finish and gloomily I voiced the thought that had been worrying me all morning. "We're going to use at least twice as much hay, oats and bran as Dad's expecting," I said. "The hay will run out in February instead of April and the oats in the bin won't last more than a couple of weeks."

"We'll have to buy some more." Penny spoke as though this were perfectly easy.

"Finance?" I asked. "We already owe Nick masses and the post office accounts are looking a bit battered."

"Christmas money," answered Penny. "The Grandfathers are certain to send us money and with any luck some of the aunts may too."

"Enough to buy a sack of oats," I admitted. "But it'll be awkward if Mum starts taking a motherly interest in what we're spending our money on and then there's still hay at an astronomic price a ton.

"The only sensible thing to do is to find them good homes," said Cathy. "Unless someone turned up who'd like to borrow Shamrock for a bit."

"No one with any sense would borrow her once they'd tried riding her," replied Penny bitterly.

The walk, trot and canter race had ended so we called to the riders that it was time to go. We explained to Nick, who didn't want to stop riding, that we'd promised to be home in time for an early lunch as our parents were taking the afternoon off to finish their Christmas shopping.

"Well, we've had the ponies all morning so you three ought to ride home," said Andrew dismounting.

"Harlequin's going superbly, Penny. Your schooling must be working at last," he added handing over the reins. Nick and Rory dismounted less willingly and Cathy and I climbed on their wet, steaming mounts. We tried to persuade Nick that it was mad for him to walk all the way to Charnworth with us when he lived in the opposite direction, but he insisted on coming. He said that he wanted to buy an airmail letter at the post office, that he might as well take Harlequin back for us and that he'd thumb a lift home; there was always quite a lot of traffic going towards Spayborne.

We stopped on the bridge to look at the river which had risen since we went up to the Firs. It was flowing very rapidly and was almost at the top of its deep-cleft banks.

"Another two inches and the floods'll be out," I observed.

"Terrific," said Andrew. "Do you remember last year and the water-splash in the park? Oh damn the F.W.," he added crossly as he remembered that we could no longer ride in the park.

Nick said, "I'm being taken shopping tomorrow morning so I don't suppose I shall see you, but if I come in the evening will someone teach me to milk?"

The girls both volunteered and I thought that it was about time Nick's friends or relations did take him shopping or something because it seemed to me that he wandered round in a very miserable and lonely way and that if we hadn't all made friends he would have been having very dreary Christmas holidays. I said, "You milk at your own risk; for goodness' sake come in your oldest clothes and prepared to be cow-kicked, beaten with a mucky tail, soaked in gallons of nutritious foamy milk and generally ill-treated." Nick said that he would and at the top of our lane we parted, leaving him to take Harlequin home.

We were in plenty of time for the earliest of lunches. We laid, mashed potatoes and made chocolate sauce while Mum changed, but, when Dad appeared he announced that shopping was off. Apparently a farm adjoining the Charnworth estate at Ashmoor had come on the market and Bird and Thatcher had offered it to the F.W. at a stiff price. "He wants to look round it this afternoon," said Dad, "and I've no intention of letting Ross have it all his own way. We could do with the extra land, it's a nice farm and it used to belong to the estate, but they're asking a sucker's price for it so I'm going along to knock a few thousands off."

Mum cursed mildly and asked if she should go to Spayborne without him, but Dad said that he'd take Wednesday morning off instead and, having bolted his lunch, he rushed off looking very cheerful at the prospect of thwarting Mr. Ross.

Mum was less cheerful. Christmas was evidently getting her down. She'd lost the list she'd made for Spayborne and all the time we were washing up she wandered about the kitchen looking in the cupboards with a dazed and desperate expression and muttering, "Friday, Saturday, Sunday, Monday, I don't suppose half the shops will open till Tuesday." And, "Oh dear, *crackers*! I knew I'd forgotten something." We decided we'd better help so we spent the afternoon making brandy butter and chestnut stuffing and arguing about who was to hunt on Boxing Day. It is traditional for us to go to the Boxing Day meet in Spayborne. Usually Cathy and I have ridden because we are the eldest and because there is another meet nearer to Charnworth on a term-time Saturday to which Conways not at boarding-schools can go, but this year I said firmly that I was too big to hunt Merlin and that it would be cruelty to ponies for Cathy to hunt Jess. At first everyone argued with me. But I pointed out that Merlin was sixteen, Jess twenty, and that my feet would catch in the jumps, and after a bit they admitted that it was true and we decided that Cathy should hunt Merlin, Andrew Jess and that Penny should ask the Brownes if she could take Harlequin, who, though no taller than Jess, is much more strongly built and in the prime of life.

Later, it actually stopped raining and Cathy and I took the ponies back and coped with Carmen. Still furious about the embrocation, she refused to be caught and we had to turn Shamrock loose and drive Carmen into the shed. Shamrock was promptly chased round the field by a squealing Jess and Carmen got so worked up that even when we had her imprisoned in the shed we still couldn't catch her. She charged about bashing Cathy and me as we tried vainly to put the halter over her horns. At last we persuaded her to eat the feed we'd brought and while she was occupied we put the halter on properly and tied her up. Unfortunately she finished her feed before we'd finished milking; then she behaved like an absolute devil, her good hind leg was permanently in the bucket and we were both soaked in milk. I was beginning to loathe the sight and the smell of the stuff, but we couldn't really blame Carmen for we both had a sneaking feeling that perhaps our milking wasn't as pro-fessional as we'd always thought it. As we turned Carmen out and fetched Shamrock in we agreed that we must do something quickly about finding a good country home. We got back to Nutsford just as Dad came in and of course we all wanted to know whether he had thwarted and subdued Mr. Ross. Dad shook his head sadly. "Mr. Smithson took the wind out of my sails before we even got there," he explained. "He said that if Ross and I started arguing we'd be there all night and he wanted to get back to his house party so would I let him have a *written* report."

"Mean," we said, and "What a lousy trick." But Dad said, "Oh well, I'm going to have my say. It was quite funny to hear young Ross boosting the place up; I must say he doesn't have much regard for the truth. I made a lot of notes," he added, producing a sheaf of papers, "Look, I'm even reduced to bringing work home from the office, that's what being employed by a financial wizard does to you. I shall have a thrombosis next."

"Was there much to pick holes in?" asked Mum.

"Woodworm in the farmhouse, dry rot in the cottages, two inconvenient rights of way – they always reduce the price a bit – and as for Ross's valuable woodland," he laughed scornfully, "a miserable little larch plantation riddled with sawfly and canker, and the rest is hardwood, mainly beech, but crooked third-rate stuff only fit for firewood."

TWELVE

The weather changed overnight and on Wednesday we wakened to a fine frosty morning, marred by a biting north-easterly wind. Mum shivered miserably and said she preferred the rain; Andrew announced that six of his toes had chilblains; Dad, departing on his early morning rounds, said thank goodness, it would dry up a bit. Penny and I put on two pullovers each and set off for the Firs. I carried Carmen's and Shamrock's breakfast over my shoulder in a sack, for we'd left the buckets up in the shed, and we ran most of the way in an attempt to warm ourselves; but the icy wind still ate deep into our bones. Shamrock was a bit cold, but more cheerful and her eyes actually lit up at the sight of her breakfast. Carmen's leg was better too; the hard frosty ground put less of a strain on it than the sloshing about in mud had done and she was able to be even more tiresome to catch. She dodged all our efforts to drive her into the shed and dashed about with her huge udder swinging and an uncomprehending expression on her face though she must have known exactly what we wanted her to do. In the end we trapped her by building a sort of funnel of poles and hurdles which narrowed to the shed entrance. Then, remembering the strains of music – mostly Radio Luxemburg – which issue from the milking parlour at Home Farm, we tried to placate her by singing as we milked. Our rather tuneless voices didn't seem to please and she cow-kicked ceaselessly, but we had become more adept at avoiding the kicks and at grabbing the bucket out of the way. While I was milking, Penny persuaded Shamrock to eat bran mixed with milk which we thought would be a very fattening diet as well as using up some of the gallons of milk we would otherwise have to chuck into the hedge every day. We were much quicker than we had been on Tuesday morning, but we were still late for breakfast; however the parents were much too taken up with writing out shopping lists and making sure they had their cheque books to notice.

By promising to wash up, put some potatoes in the oven to bake, and make the house reasonably tidy before Mrs. Toms, who was coming to do some housework, arrived, we got the parents off to Spayborne in good time. Then we rushed around doing chores at speed and afterwards we ate apples and read the newspapers until Mrs. Toms came. We gave her Mum's countless messages, left Andrew and Rory in the Old Kitchen playing with the electric train and, feeling rather pleased at the thought of a ride without responsibilities we collected caps and gloves. Coats simply wouldn't fit over our numerous pullovers so we all had to go out muffled in macintoshes though it was a fine day; pullovers alone are misery in a wind. As soon as Cathy and I had groomed and saddled up we rode round to the Old Rectory to collect Penny and for once she wasn't ready. As we stood waiting for her in the sunniest spot in the cobbled stable yard, Mrs. Browne bore down upon us, giving excitable cries. "Don't tell me it's true," she said, "I don't believe anyone could be such a fiend especially at Christmas. Oh, it's too awful; poor Fiona."

I suppose we looked as startled as we felt, because she broke off absuptly. "Oh dear, don't say I've put my foot in it," she cried. "Don't say you haven't been told."

"Told what?" I asked. I was pleased that my voice sounded calm, even casual, disguising the horrible churning fright that was going on inside me.

"I don't know that I ought to repeat it," fussed Mrs. Browne, "but I heard from my 'daily' who heard it from her niece, who's married to one of the gardeners at the house, so she *ought* to know what she's talking about, though I must say I *do* disapprove of gossip and in the general way I *never* repeat it; well, she heard that your poor father had, had – was leaving and Mr. Smithson was taking on that Mr. Ross instead. I don't believe it; it would be too awful," she gushed, "after all these years and you all love the place so."

Suddenly I realised that I disliked Mrs. Browne. I disliked her too bright, too elaborately arranged hair; her tight London clothes, her gush and the excitement she was getting out of this rumour that Dad had been given the push.

"Well, it hadn't happened at nine-thirty this morning," I told her in rather a cold voice. "But I suppose it *could* happen any time. Meanwhile it's like the factory at Ashmoor and the drilling for oil – just another rumour."

"Oh, I'm so glad," breathed Mrs. Browne with false or at least over-emphasised relief. "I was sure he couldn't be *such* a fiend. I didn't think that even a billionaire could do such a thing at *Christmas*." Mercifully, at this moment Penny appeared.

"We'll tell Mum to ring you up if there's any news," said Cathy brightly as we rode across the yard. "Goodbye," we called as we rode out of the Old Rectory gate.

Cathy and I looked at each other and both our faces said "don't let's tell Penny". I contented myself by saying "That woman gets on my nerves."

"And mine," agreed Cathy.

"And mine. Where are we going?" asked Penny.

"Charnworth Down," I suggested. "I feel like a gallop." I did too. I wanted to gallop away from Mrs. Browne's gush and Mr. Ross's desire to be the Charnworth agent. I wanted to forget that the F.W. held all our fates in his money-grabbing hand. I wanted to still small nagging fears about what we'd do if we left Charnworth or where we'd go.

It was bitterly cold on the down and the ponies were very willing to gallop, so we galloped as fast and as far as they could. Speed acted with its usual magic on my black mood and afterwards as we rode down the chalk track from the hill, things seemed brighter; the oil, the factory and the housing estate had all been baseless rumours, why not this as well? I turned in my saddle to make an optimistic face at Cathy. On the bridge we stopped to look at the Spay; it was just about to burst its banks. On our side of the road and river the ground rises steeply and forces the flood water over the other bank where the lower slopes of Charnworth Down rise from brown osiers and marshy woodland. But on the other side of the road lie the water meadows: Bridge Meadow, Brook Meadow, where the Charnworth brook vainly trying to join the over-full Spay lay stagnant, but still within its brimming banks, and beyond them the Meads. A hunched, cold-looking heron was fishing, standing in some shallow water on long legs. I could hear a tractor at work on the higher ground behind the village; probably, I thought, they'd found a field dry enough to plough.

Then I heard a thin cry, it sounded like "Douglas", but it was snatched away by a gust of wind before I was certain. The others had heard something too; we all listened. In a lull the cry came again, plainly this time, "Douglas, Penny, Cathy, come quickly." It sounded like Rory's voice. We looked around anxiously trying to see him, casting apprehensive glances at the river. Suddenly we saw him. "Look!" cried Cathy pointing. And I exclaimed, "Oh Lord! The ricks." We could see two figures waving frantically from the rickyard two fields away from us and behind them rose an ominous spiral of grey smoke.

THIRTEEN

Across country there were three gates and the brook; it would be quicker by road, I thought. I turned Merlin and set off at a gallop keeping as much on the grass verge as I could. Cathy and Penny thundered behind. We tore round the bend in the road past our lane. Merlin never hesitated, he had sensed the urgency of the moment, and swung down the short lane that leads to the rickyard. I leapt off, flung open the double five-barred gates, led Merlin in and threw his reins over the fence. Then I ran between the ricks round the Dutch barn towards the smoke. Cathy and Penny were on my heels. The stretch of loose straw between the Dutch barn and the post and rails which fenced the rickyard from the fields was alight and Rory and Nick were stamping on the flames, but all the time the blaze was spreading, creeping nearer and nearer to the huge barn crammed with hay and straw and the ricks beyond it; some of them of still unthreshed oats. "What shall we do?" they cried, stamping desperately in the cloud of grey smoke while the area of the fire grew larger with every second, orange tongues licking evilly among the golden straw.

"Are there any forks or brooms about?" I asked

looking round anxiously as I tore off Dad's army surplus garment. "Go and look, Rory," I said, throwing it down on a patch of flames and stamping on it.

"There's a water-trough," Cathy told me. "Can you find anything to carry water in?" I asked, turning to smother another rush of flames fanned to life by a gust of wind.

"Riding hats," cried Penny, she snatched mine off my head and she and Cathy disappeared round the barn. A tear-streaked, fire-blackened Rory came flying up with a pitchfork. "Give it to Nick," I told him, without looking up from my flame-smothering efforts. "Nick," I yelled, "clear a fire-break between the flames and the barn. Clear all the straw off a strip about six feet wide." Nick darted behind me and began to fork straw in frenzied haste. The girls came running with hatfuls of water which they poured on the flames already out-flanking me. "We had to break the ice," called Cathy breathlessly as she rushed away.

Rory appeared with another fork, a four-pronged one, which I seized gladly as the army surplus garment had had just about disintegrated. I began to fork back the flames.

"We didn't mean to do it. We only wanted to get warm," sobbed Rory. "Nick thought it would be all right." Absolute horror took hold of me. "You don't mean to say you started it?" I cried unbelievingly as I beat and forked at the flames. A glance at his frightened face, black except where a torrent of tears had washed two clean strips, told me the worst. "Go and help the girls," I yelled at him angrily. I couldn't stop to consider all the awful consequences; the fire was gaining on us. I beat and forked and stamped. It was terribly hot. My eyes were smarting with the smoke and the sweat was pouring off me. The girls appeared again and again with hats of water, but still the blaze grew. I'd held it back in front but now it spread sideways and completely outflanked me, and suddenly there were two arms of fire advancing on the barn. I called to Nick to help and together we forked and beat, running up and down before the barn, hurling back flaming forkfuls of straw on to the spent, blackened ashes behind. It seemed that we would never hold it. The venomous orange tongues crept and raced and smouldered and all the time they multiplied, licking round us, shooting up where we least expected them, drawing nearer to the barn. We ought to send for the fire brigade, I thought desperately, it's beating us. But we couldn't spare anyone while there was still a chance, and we couldn't admit that Rory had set fire to a rickyard – the agent's son – it didn't bear thinking about. I redoubled my efforts. I stamped and beat and hurled. The girls seemed to have got the water organised. They began to appear more often. Cathy had a bucket. It leaked, I noticed, but it held more than the hat she carried in her other hand. They ran backwards and forwards across the hot ashes and poured their water wherever the flames were beating us back. Then there always seemed to be a girl pouring water and suddenly the flames grew less. We fought on, filled with a rising hope. The flames grew less and less gradually one by one the last orange tongues sizzled and died down, on the very edge of Nick's firebreak, six feet from the barn.

A feeling of relief swept over me. "Thank God!" I said, leaning on my fork, and I really meant it. We looked round us at the oblong desert of ashes from the rickyard fence to the barn. The smoke had blown away with the wind, but the acrid smell of wet ash was strong. Nick and I scraped about looking for smouldering pockets, the girls threw more water to make sure. We were all reluctant to discuss what we must do next, but it had to come. I wiped my sweat-grimed face on the cuff of my pullover and turned on Nick. "How could you be so absolutely crazy?" I demanded.

"We were cold," he answered avoiding my eye. "We never thought it would spread."

"In a rickyard, in this wind? And you never thought it would spread?" I was angry. The fright we'd had and the thought of the complications ahead were all Nick's fault. I wasn't going to temper my scorn. "You must be absolutely half-witted," I said. Nick scraped the ashes, still avoiding my eye. Rory was crying. Cathy came across with a bucket of water. She looked at me white-faced. "Douglas," she said in a strangled sort of voice, "I think the F.W.'s here."

I just stood. I couldn't think of anything else to do. I remained leaning on my fork with fear churning in my stomach and making me hot and cold by turn, until two men appeared round the barn. One, large, camel-coated and bespectacled was obviously the F.W., the other, I supposed, was Mr. Ross.

Cathy stood beside me white-faced, Rory huddled between us sobbing bitterly and Penny came across the ashes and poured her last load of water before joining us, a dripping riding hat in either hand. The F.W. looked from the ashes to the barn and then at me. "What happened?" he asked. There was nothing for it but the truth. I had to swallow a lump in my throat before I could answer. "I'm afraid my brother and . . ." I looked round for Nick and found he had disappeared – "my brother and another boy started a fire because they were cold. They didn't realise it would spread. When it did they saw us on the bridge and yelled for help." My voice trained away. Rory's sobs filled the silence.

"Where's the other boy?" asked the F.W. We all looked round. It didn't seem possible that Nick could have run and left us to face the F.W., but there was no sign of him. "He seems to have sloped off," I said bitterly. "He's older, he ought to have had more sense. Rory's only eight."

"You're the Conways, aren't you?" asked the F.W. And we admitted it, wishing that we were almost anybody else on earth.

Then Mr. Ross took a hand. "I don't suppose there was another boy," he said, "they've just thought that up on the spur of the moment; it's a case of arson pure and simple, and the place for that young man," he pointed at Rory, "is the police station."

Rory's howls grew louder. He grabbed Cathy's hand as though he expected to be dragged away from us. I'd have taken anything from the F.W. but it wasn't Ross's ricks we'd nearly burned down. I turned on him fiercely. "There was another boy," I said. "We're not liars; and the only thing we thought of on the spur of the moment was how to put the fire out."

"And you're not taking Rory to the police station." Cathy spoke quietly but you could tell she meant it.

Mr. Ross looked furious, his smooth, round, rather chinless face turned red, "I'm not taking any cheek from you," he shouted. "You're nothing but a gang of young thugs. You've nearly burned down five thousand pounds' worth of ricks and then you say it isn't arson. We'll have the lot of you in the Juvenile Court."

I started to shout back, but Penny's voice cut in, calm and cool as ice. "We've done absolutely no damage at all," she said, "so I don't know what you're shouting about." This really set Ross off. I made a face at Penny trying to tell her to keep out of it; she nearly always makes rows worse.

"You ruddy kids," Ross was shouting. "You think you can do exactly as you like . . ."

And the F.W. was trying to quieten him down. "Ross," he said, "leave it. Ross, I'll deal with this." Mr. Ross stormed on, "No respect for property, treat the place as though it belongs to you, you think you'll get away with it just because you're Conway kids, but this time you won't."

"You can leave my father out of it," I yelled, working myself up into a melodramatic mood.

"And that's just what I'm not going to do," Ross yelled back.

The F.W. turned on me. "That's enough of this," he said curtly. "Take your little brother home." Rory tried to stammer out something about being sorry and not having meant to, but the F.W. cut him short. "All right," he said, "now go on home."

Penny retrieved the third riding hat from the fence. I jabbed at the ashes with my fork. "This oughtn't to be left," I said, "it may flare up again."

"I'll see to it," answered the F.W. and then as Ross opened his mouth to speak the F.W. roared at me, "Will you go HOME!"

"I'm going," I answered. I stuck my pitchfork in the ground, gave Ross what I hoped was a withering look and followed the others round the Dutch barn.

Merlin and Jess were waiting patiently, but Harlequin

had broken his reins and was helping himself from one of the ricks. "Better not let Mr. Ross see that," I observed jauntily, my blood was still up. Cathy put Rory on Jess, but the rest of us decided to walk. Leading the ponies and carrying our soaking riding hats under our arms, we squeezed past the silver-grey Bentley parked outside the rickyard gates and turned for home. My blood began to go down to its normal temperature. The excitement of the yelling match with Mr. Ross departed; the awful fact that Rory had nearly burned down the F.W.'s ricks, and that Dad had to be told, remained. If the rumours were true, I comforted myself, nothing we did would make much difference, but I couldn't drive away the feeling that if Dad's job had been hanging in the balance, we'd tipped the scales right over. If only we'd kept our mouths shut, I thought, if we'd let Mr. Ross bawl us out things might not have been so bad; answering back got you nowhere. And then there was Nick.

Cathy was trying to calm Rory down. "You were silly," she said, "that's all. You didn't mean to set fire to anything and you had the sense to call us. It was much more Nick's fault than yours."

"He's only a town boy," sobbed Rory, "he doesn't know about ricks and winds and things."

"He's a beast," said Penny fiercely. "How *could* he run off like that and leave us to do all the explaining— I'm never going to speak to him again."

"We thought he was such a friend," added Cathy sadly. I couldn't think of any reasonable explanation for him leaving us in the lurch, especially when he knew how terribly important it was for us to be on good terms with the F.W. Nick de Veriac and the smallest Conway would have seemed so much less serious than the

"Conway kids". We'd all liked him and we'd let him into so many of our secrets; it seemed very bitter that he should have done this to us and it would have seemed even more bitter if it hadn't been overshadowed by the larger and more frightening issue of Dad's job. We saw with a feeling of relief that there was no Land-Rover parked outside the front door. The parents weren't back and that meant a brief reprieve. We put the ponies in the stable, watered and fed them. I looked at my watch; it was twenty minutes to one. "We'd better clean our-selves up," I said, looking from Rory who was black from head to foot, to the girls who'd escaped with smears. We went in through the back door and horrified Mrs. Toms who seemed to be turning out the larder. We felt too dispirited to explain things to her so Cathy said we must wash before Mum saw us and we escaped to the cloakroom and began to kick off black and sticky shoes and take stock of the damage. My riding gloves were a total loss, my socks had small charred holes all round the ankles and my hands were a mass of small burns and blisters. The girls and Rory were wet as well as grimy, and Rory had a burn on one of his hands that was worse than any of mine. We tried to dandy brush each other down, but it didn't work and we all had to change. Afterwards Cathy did our burns up with lint and sticking plaster and I sent Penny to find Andrew and tell him what had happened.

When Andrew appeared he was tactful; he main-tained a dismal silence and helped to lay lunch. Mrs. Toms had gone home. We'd just finished laying and were wondering what do to next when we heard the Land Rover coming up the lane. We all went to the front door to help carry in the shopping. The parents were full of good cheer. They unloaded and handed us parcels with cries of "don't feel that" and "no peeping". Put everything in the sitting-room." Mum told us, "I'll sort it out after lunch." By the time they were indoors they'd realised that something was wrong. "What's the matter?" asked Mum looking puzzled. "You all seem very glum."

"Something awful happened," I said. And Rory promptly burst into tears. "Rory and Nick lit a fire by the Home Farm rickyard," I rushed on determined to get it over, "the wind caught it and it spread, but they yelled to the rest of us who were riding and between us we put it out before it reached the Dutch barn or the ricks. Only Mr. Smithson and Mr. Ross turned up and there was a bit of a row."

"On, *no*!" exclaimed Mum, and Dad clasped his head with both hands and gave a groan.

"It didn't actually do any damage," said Penny tactlessly.

"No damage," Dad almost shrieked. "When the agent's son practically sets fire to his employer's rick? What was Rory doing out alone, anyway?"

We looked at each other. "Well, when Mrs. Toms came we went riding and left him and Andrew playing with the train," I answered. Andrew looked embarrassed. "Nick turned up," he said, "he played with the train for a bit and then he wanted to go out and well, Rory would go too."

We all knew what this meant. Andrew pleading and Rory telling him to go to the devil; we'd all heard it happen dozens of times before. No one could blame Andrew.

"Then what happened, Rory?" asked Dad.

"We walked about for a bit," Rory stammered between sobs, "and then we were cold and Nick said why not light a fire? He had some matches and we collected sticks and some straw and lit it in the corner of the rickyard. It was only a little fire at first and then the wind blew it and it went everywhere. Nick didn't know what to do and then I saw Douglas and Cathy and Penny on the bridge so we called and called and they came galloping and put it out."

"And then Mr. Smithson and Ross turned up?" asked Dad bitterly.

"Yes," I took over the story. "Mr. Smithson was quite nice at first, but Mr. Ross started yelling at us and threatening to take Rory to the police station, so we, well we yelled back," I admitted sadly. "Then Nick had run off so they didn't really believe there had been an older boy and it was all pretty disagreeable. Finally Mr. Smithson told us to take Rory home."

"Rory said he was sorry," added Cathy, "to Mr. Smithson, I mean."

Dad was sitting on the arm of a chair and Mum had collapsed on the sofa amid the piles of parcels. They sat looking miserable and only Rory's sobs broke the silence. Then Dad sighed and looked at his watch. "We'd better have lunch," he said. We made for the door, but Mum called after us, "Douglas, what have you done to your hands?"

"Burned them," I answered, "but they're not bad; Rory's got a worse one."

Mum rushed to inspect Rory and even Dad relented enough to tell him to stop crying as what was done was done. The rest of us hurried about fetching plates and butter and cold meat and baked potatoes in an unnaturally helpful way.

No one ate much lunch. Rory sniffed, Dad was gloomily preoccupied and Mum passed things feverishly and offered second helpings which we all refused; it had been difficult enough to force the first helping down. As Dad swallowed his last mouthful he glanced at his watch and announced that he must be off. Cathy and I looked at each other. We knew jolly well where he was going. Poor Dad, I thought, and I began to feel angry with Rory and angrier still with Nick.

We washed up drearily and then Mum persuaded Penny and Andrew to play a car-racing game with Rory; when they'd departed to the Old Kitchen Cathy and I offered to help her. We carried parcels and presents upstairs to the spare bedroom, edibles to the kitchen and crackers and dates and oranges and lemon slices to the dining-room. Mum tried to cheer us up. She showed us the camel-coloured waistcoat she'd bought for Dad; he'd wanted one for ages, and his present from Storm, a very superior key-ring. When the parcels were all in their appropriate spots we asked what else we could do and Mum said that if we really wanted to be useful we could mince the rest of the joint up for shepherd's pie. So Cathy and I retired to the kitchen and minced. We minced with energy, mentally substituting Mr. Ross and the F.W. and Nick for mutton. Then, when at last we heard the Land Rover returning, we abandoned a half-minced onion, which had reduced us both to tears, and dashed into the hall, Mum had beaten us to it. "Well?" she asked Dad.

"He was quite nice about it," Dad answered leading the way into the sitting-room. "First of all I went and had a look at the rickyard," he winced at the recollection. "I expected a sort of bonfire-sized patch, but the area of ashes is bigger than this room. Another six feet and the Dutch barn would have gone up. It was such a near thing it doesn't bear thinking about. You ought to have sent for the fire brigade," he added, turning to me.

"I nearly did, but we couldn't really spare anyone. I think if we had the fire would have reached the barn; we only just kept it back," I explained.

"All right," said Dad, "if it was a calculated risk."

"I thought of the fire brigade too," Cathy told us. "It seemed the only thing to do when we found that the ballcock of the water-trough was frozen and there was no water coming, but Penny kicked it and then water simply gushed out. After that there wasn't time to think, we just ran backwards and forwards with water. We put Rory in the field and he filled the riding hats and handed them over the fence, but the bucket was rather heavy and I had to help with that."

"It was Rory who found the pitchforks too," I added, feeling that a word in his favour would do no harm. "I sent him to look while I tried to smother the flames with – oh Lord—" I broke off. "Dad, I'm terribly sorry, but that army surplus garment of yours is no more. I used it for smothering flames until it disintegrated and Rory produced the forks."

"That's all right. I'd willingly sacrifice my entire wardrobe to save the Dutch barn, quite apart from the ricks," Dad answered. "What about this friend of yours – Nick –did he help?"

"Oh yes, he cleared a firebreak until things got quite out of control and then he helped with the main blaze. We couldn't possibly have put it out without him. He didn't slope off until he saw the F.W. coming."

"Do tell us exactly what Mr. Smithson said," Mum asked Dad.

"Well, I drove up to the house and asked to see him," answered Dad, "and I was taken into a room full of people. He seems to have his whole family staying there for Christmas. He must have known very well why I'd come, but he insisted on introducing me all round. Mother, aunt, sister, brother-in-law, nephew, all the lot. I asked to see him along for a minute and he said, "Look Conway, let's forget it, shall we? The older children put the fire out very promptly; no damage was done and the little boy will never do it again. Supposing we drop the subject?' I tried to say my piece, but he wouldn't listen. 'Forget it', he said. Then he offered me a cigarette and made me talk to his brother-in-law who's trying to get rid of a tenant under the Bad Husbandry clause of the 1958 Agriculture Act."

Mum sighed with relief. "Thank heavens for that," she said. "And perhaps he's not such an ogre after all."

"He was certainly nice enough," agreed Dad. "In fact he couldn't really have been nicer, but there are two ways of looking at it. He was a bit impersonal about it all and that made me wonder if he'd decided on making a certain change and so, of course, there was no point in kicking up about Rory. I can't tell what he's thinking. He's always quiet and polite and he nearly always wears that same inscrutable expression. I just don't understand him; I only wish I did."

Mum sighed again and this time it wasn't with relief. If Dad thought we didn't know what he meant by a certain change he was wrong. I toyed with the idea of telling him about Mrs. Browne's rumour, but I decided against it. Time along would show, I thought dismally, and there was no point in adding to Dad's worries.

"I'd better tell Rory Mr. Smithson's forgiven him," observed Dad going to the door, "and then I really must go and do some work. I think he's been frightened enough, don't you?" he asked Mum. "I don't think I need say any more."

"No, except that I don't think Nick is a very suitable person for him to go out alone with," answered Mum. "Tell him he's not to go off like that again. Even Andrew would know not to light a fire in a rickyard."

FOURTEEN

On Thursday morning, the morning of Christmas Eve, Cathy and I watched a red sun rise over Sutton's Hill as we made our way to the Firs.

" 'Red morning, shepherd's warning'," said Cathy. "I hope it goes over; we don't want snow or rain for Boxing Day."

Locally it is supposed that if a red sky goes over and dies away in the west the shepherds can refrain from panic. But this one didn't go over; by the time we'd milked – Cathy had to do most of it because my hands were in such a mess — our red sky was sinking steadily back into the east.

As we rode homewards we discussed advertising Carmen. We decided that as soon as Christmas was over we'd send an advertisement to the *Spayborne and District Gazette* and we'd pay extra and have a box number so that no one would be able to telephone us and we'd only have to waylay the postman each morning to collect the replies. We were feeling quite optimistic by the time we reached home and, thanks to Cathy's speedy milking, we were more or less in time for breakfast. We burst into the dining-room cheerfully and collided with an absolute fog of gloom.

"What's the matter?" I asked.

"Nothing really," answered Mum. "It's just Andrew being idiotic."

"Rumours again," said Dad, getting up to put his egg plate on the sideboard. "When young Barry Toms brought the newspapers he asked Andrew if it was true I'd been fired."

"I don't *want* to leave Nutsford," Andrew burst out, tears falling into his egg. Rory was sniffing and Penny said, "I could kill that beastly Smithson," in a ferocious voice.

"Oh, Andrew darling, don't," begged Mum. "There's no point in making yourself miserable over something that may never happen."

"After all it wasn't true about the oil drilling or the bungalows or the factory at Ashmoor," I told him offering my own particular crumb of comfort.

"And surely Mr. Smithson would tell you first, wouldn't he, Dad?" asked Cathy.

"Yes, of course he would," Dad answered. "Andrew, stop it. Come on, dry up. Now look, all of you," he went on, "are we going to let Mr. Smithson spoil our Christmas? Because that's what he's going to do if you all go on like this. Supposing we ban him? No one allowed to mention him or even think about him until Boxing Day; a complete ban?"

"Like swearing," said Rory cheering up at once and beginning to bounce about in his chair. "Smithson's a rude and wicked word like damn and hell and bloody—"

"Shut up," I told him hastily. Rory knows far more swear words than I did at eight and I didn't think that this was the moment for him to disclose his whole lurid vocabulary. Luckily the parents were more interested in Andrew who'd borrowed a handkerchief and was blowing his nose in a determined manner.

"Well," Dad asked. "Do you all agree?"

We all agreed dutifully and Dad turned to Mum. "You'll have to keep them up to it, Fi," he said, "because you're not going to see much of me today. I've got this Research Officer from the Forestry Commission coming and I'll have to take him round myself. Trust a civil servant to choose Christmas Eve. Still, I've got an axe to grind," he went on as he got up from the table. "I hear they've got some first-class ash seed at the Research Station and I want to get hold of a few pounds to sow in our nursery. Then, in two or three years' time, when we clear fell the coppice at Ashmoor, I'll have some decent trees for replanting instead of" – he broke off suddenly and from the dismal look which crossed his face, I knew he was thinking that we were unlikely to be at Nutsford in three years' time. "Well, see you at tea," he said with forced heartiness and went out.

"And what are you all going to do?" asked Mum brightly.

"First aid needed, please," I said exhibiting my hands. "Practically all the blisters have burst and I'm a soggy mess."

"So am I," cried Rory, Mum was shocked by our hands. She removed us to the bathroom, applied appropriate ointments and copious bandages and forbade us to do anything that would get them wet.

The riding turns were in a hopeless muddle and partly to sort things out and partly because of our hands Rory and I said we would forego our turns for the moment;

the others decided to go for a short ride and then clean the tack ready for Boxing Day. Mum said that Rory could help her and I, feeling tired and middle-aged, decided to read. I collected two apples, a book from the sitting-room shelves, and retired to the Old Kitchen. I lit the oil heater, settled myself in the more comfortable arm-chair with my feet on the other one, and relaxed. I felt rather invalidish when I heard the ponies and riders depart, but then I became absorbed in my book and oblivious of everything else until about three-quarters of an hour later when the side door opened quietly and Nick slid into the room.

"Hullo," I said, looking up. And then, remembering the fire, "What do you want?"

Nick stayed by the door. "I came to say I was sorry about yesterday." His voice was harsh and he looked away from me. "I didn't mean to run out on you; it just sort of happened. I think I expected you to run too."

"It's not much use us running in Charnworth," I answered. "We're too well known."

"Yes, I didn't think of that until afterwards. What happened?" His voice took on a pleading note. "Was there an awful row?"

"Yes, there was a bit of a slanging match," I answered. "We explained that it was an accident; that you and Rory had lit the fire to warm yourselves and it had got out of control. But Ross said you didn't exist and Rory had committed arson and he wanted to take him to the police station. We all lost our tempers and yelled until the F.W. got fed up and told us to go home. Afterwards, Dad went up to see him and he was very nice about it and said to drop the subject. But the village is full of rumours that Dad is going to get the push," I went on wearily, "so we think that perhaps the F.W. thought Rory wasn't worth bothering about." Now it was I who was avoiding Nick's eyes and trying to keep my voice matter of fact.

Nick came nearer. "I'll go and see him and explain the whole thing. I'll tell him it was all my fault — that's true. Rory hadn't even any matches — I'll go and see him this morning," he offered, "if you think it'll do any good."

"I don't know whether it would or not," I answered wearily. "The F.W. said forget it, Dad's banned any mention of the Smithsons until Boxing Day. I just don't know, Nick, you'd better do whatever you think." If Nick wanted to be heroic and do a sort of *Four Feathers*, A. E. W. Mason act of confronting the danger he'd run from, I wasn't going to stop him, but I couldn't see much sense in him doing it for the Conways; a feeling in my bones told me that: as far as the F.W. was concerned, we'd reached the point of no return.

"Is Penny livid with me?" asked Nick picking out the pattern on the back of the other arm-chair.

"Yes, she is rather," I answered. "Yesterday she was never going to speak to you again, but probably she'll relent," I spoke casually; I was becoming a bit bored with Nick's intenseness.

"Tell her I'm sorry, will you?" asked Nick.

"Oh, for heaven's sake, Nick, forget it!" I said, adopting the F.W.'s attitude. "Dad's right, we're all going to have an absolutely miserable Christmas if we go on like this." Then, as he showed no sign of taking himself off, I went on, "If you've nothing better to do you can help me with the decorating. Can you paste paper chains? These bandages make me so clumsy, I can't do a thing."

Nick said he hadn't anything else to do, so I found the packets of paper-chain strips and the paste and, since he appeared clueless, explained how to make them. Then we sat at the table and while he pasted we talked about general subjects like school and Christmas. Nick had spent last Christmas in a London hotel, one of the very grand ones. He didn't seem to have enjoyed it much and I soon realised that he didn't look forward to it or have half the fun that we do. Altogether I felt sorry for him. It's all very well for Andrew to want exciting relations, but it's not much fun if they go off on secret missions the whole time and leave you to wander about alone. When he'd used up all six packets of strips we hung the paper chains, or rather Nick did. I was reduced to handing and holding. We put the four best ones in the dining-room and the rest criss-crossed the Old Kitchen in glorious confusion. The sitting-room is discreetly decorated with a few sprigs of holly and Christmas cards on strings, usually by Mum.

"Now there's only the holly," I said. "We'll get that this afternoon." But Nick wasn't listening to me. He'd heard the clatter of hoofs in the lane and, looking rather shame-faced, he said he must go. I took pity on him and let him out of the front door as soon as the others were safely in the yard. Then I went to tell them what had happened and I met them in the kitchen passage as they came in carrying their tack.

"Nick turned up," I told them. "He's very sorry he ran off yesterday; he says he doesn't know why he did it. He offered to go and tell the F.W. it was all his fault. I said he could if he liked, but that officially the subject was dropped."

Mum's head appeared round the kitchen door. "I am glad," she said. "We thought we heard him, at least Rory said that was who it was."

"Poor Nick, was he very miserable about it?" asked Cathy.

"Yes, he seemed a bit desperate," I answered. "I put him on to making paper chains and then he cheered up, but he did a very rapid bunk when he heard you come back."

"You don't mean you've made it up with him, just like that?" asked Penny in incredulous tones. "That you're going to be friends with him again as though nothing had happened?"

"Well, he said he was sorry," I pointed out.

"So he jolly well ought to be," said Penny, "running off and leaving us to explain things like that. I'm never going to speak to him again even if you do."

"Oh, Penny," we chorused disapprovingly. Penny set her jaw stubbornly. "I think you're feeble, making it up just because he says he's sorry."

Mum's head appeared round the kitchen door again. "But Penny, you do silly things sometimes and regret them afterwards," she said.

"I don't run off when I've started a fire and leave other people to take the blame," answered Penny.

"No, because flapping in emergencies isn't one of your faults," argued Mum emerging into the kitchen passage, "but that doesn't mean you haven't got any."

"I still think he's mean and cowardly and if I meet him I shall cut him," said Penny in uncompromising tones and she stumped off down the passage.

Mum looked after her, a worried frown on her face.

"She'll get over it," I said.

"I shall speak to Nick," announced Andrew. "After all he's said he's sorry and I hate rows that go on and on."

"So shall I," agreed Rory. "I expect he was just afraid. I should have run when the F.W. came if Cathy and Douglas hadn't been there."

"If you're going to clean the tack before lunch, you'd better hurry up," said Mum reappearing. "You've only got half an hour." Andrew rushed off saying he'd never get his done in that time and I shouted after him that he must; there was the holly to get and the ponies to take back before the Carol Service at five o'clock.

Somehow getting the holly wasn't as much fun as usual and, despite Dad's ban the F.W. kept cropping up. We couldn't visit the best bushes by the Quarry in Castle Woods because of him, so we cut some very mediocre stuff from the bushes by the track to Charnworth Down and then we saw some ivy in one of the spinneys and as Penny said even a financial wizard couldn't really object to people removing parasitic growths from his trees, so we removed it, but Andrew and Rory were in a state of nervous dread lest he should come and catch us and shook in their shoes as they kept watch.

Then there was Carmen to milk and the girls took the ponies back to the Firs while the rest of us finished the decorations and fetched in the huge logs for the Old Kitchen fire and some normal-sized ones for the sitting-room. We cleaned ourselves up and had tea peacefully but Cathy and Penny had a terrible rush. They were hardly in the house before the bells began to ring and we had to feed them with bread and butter and jam as they changed and they ate their cake as we hurried along the lane. As we turned into the back drive Andrew said, "Supposing *he's* there?"

"We say good evening," Cathy told him. "He won't eat us." Rory began to giggle. "He might. Roast Andrew with Malteser stuffing." Cathy said, "Shush." And I pointed out, "With any luck we won't meet him face to face. The church is always pretty full and there's safety in numbers."

"I should like to cut him," said Penny.

"Well, you can't," I told her. "And after all he was nice about the fire, at least he was to Dad." The roar he'd given me still rankled. Then we came round the bend in the drive and the church stood before us. Light poured from the high windows illuminating short grass and grey tombstones and black pyramidal yews.

"Doesn't it look romantic," said Cathy.

"Like a Christmas card," agreed Andrew. And Rory added, "If only it would snow." We stood for a moment looking at the scene and then everyone else seemed to be hurrying in and the five-minute bell was ringing; we went in too. The pew where we usually sit and the Charnworth family pew were empty but otherwise the church was full. Cathy and I made Rory sit between us because he's been known to put things down Andrew's neck during a dull sermon, and almost at once the bell stopped and the service began. We had nearly all our favourite carols. We prefer the noisy ones as then the rather tuneless Conway singing is drowned, and it was in the middle of "Hark the Herald Angels Sing" that Rory, who'd been wriggling for some time, whispered that the F.W. was there, at the back, I silenced him with a furious look and controlled my desire to look round. But when the service was over, I decided that a rapid

exit with the main throng would be safest. Not that it
was a rapid exit, it was more of a snail's pace procession
for the vicar stood at the door shaking hands with everyone. Outside we were surrounded by friends from the
village. Some of them wished us a happy Christmas and I
felt sure from the sympathetic looks on their faces,
ghostly in the dim light, that they were thinking that this
would be our last Christmas at Charnworth. Dave
Bishop, the gamekeeper's son, asked me why he hadn't
seen me these holidays and Mrs. Broome, surrounded by
her six children, asked what we'd been doing with
ourselves, they'd missed us, she sai1, down in the village.
We couldn't explain either that Carmen's never-ending
needs kept us busier than usual or that curious ques-
tioners and commiserating looks made us keep clear of
the village. We answered evasively and began to wish
people Merry Christmas in rather loud voices. Several
of the older people came up to ask "How Mother was
keeping?" and I thought I detected a ghoul-like interest
in their voices. But once you begin to expect pity you
seem to see it everywhere; plain from the good-natured,
blended with curiosity from the inquisitive and mixed
with perverted pleasure from the ghouls. I decided that
my judgement was becoming warped and noticing that
the others had glided off I began edging my way out of
the crowd. Looking round I caught the F.W.'s eye.
"Good evening, sir," I said loudly and made a dash for
the protective darkness of the back drive. I found the
others giggling apprehensively in the shadows. "He was
pointing us out to Mrs. F.W.," Penny told me. "We
thought you were going to get caught."

"Are you sure it was Mrs. F.W.?" asked Andrew.

"Not sure," answered Penny, "but she looked as

though she might be."

"But she wasn't a *bit* fabulous," complained Andrew in disappointed tones.

"Poor Andrew expected ermine or mink," observed Cathy.

"And white satin and lashings of diamonds and fabulous grass-green eye shadow," I suggested.

"He expected to see a fairy princess," lisped Rory mockingly. "You're barmy, mate," he added, pushing Andrew.

"Actually," said Penny, "she didn't look too bad."

"I wish I'd seen her," I grumbled.

"Well, she has fairish, sort of curly hair," said Cathy, "and she was wearing a brown and white check coat. She looks smart, but not in the townish way that Mrs. Browne does. And she's younger than the F.W. About forty something, I should think."

"Oh, older than that," argued Penny. "Mum's thirty-nine."

My mind had left the Smithsons and I was remembering other Christmas Eves when, after the Carol Service some of us were invited into the oak-panelled hall of Charnworth House to eat mince pies. Old Lord Charnworth had always called me David, but sometimes he'd tipped me a pound or two, and even if he'd laughed pointlessly and too often, and his jokes had been made again and again, his jovial manner had been a lot better than the ominous silence and inscrutable glances of the F.W.

Suddenly I felt sad. The joyful rejoicing spirit of the carols faded away and I could only think that this was probably our last Christmas at Charnworth. "For heaven's sake shine that torch on the lane, Andrew," I snapped disagreeably, "I've just fallen into my eighth puddle."

When we reached home we found Dad in the hall, decorating a Christmas tree in rather a dispirited manner. When he saw us he at once became hearty. "It's the top of a Douglas fir," he told us, "they were thinning and the rest of the tree's going for pit poles. I'd rather have a top than one of the young trees, they hardly ever survive the heat indoors and it always seems like murder to me. How did the carols go?"

"Fine," we answered, and "Great, terrific."

"The F.W. was there," said Andrew, "and somebody who may be Mrs. F.W., but she wasn't a bit fabulous."

"Banned!" yelled Rory. "Banned, banned, banned!"

"Oh, shut up," Andrew told him, "you've been talking about them."

"That was different; we couldn't help it; we saw them. Now they're banned again. Banned, banned, banned!" yelled Rory.

Andrew hit out at him and Rory hit back and in a moment they were rolling over and over on the floor, sloshing each other in a very bad-tempered way.

"Stop it," yelled Dad. Penny and I grabbed bits of them and pulled them apart, but they were very angry and struggled to get at each other again. Mum appeared from the sitting-room. "Bed," she said. "Go on, Rory, have a bath and mind you wash. Go on. Hurry up or Father Christmas won't come," she threatened.

"Don't believe in him," said Rory going upstairs backwards and as slowly as possible. "I know it's only you and Dad."

The rest of us were shooed to bed at ungodly hours with irritating threats about Father Christmas. And it was all nonsense because the parents always go to the Midnight Mass and do the stockings when they get back, and that wasn't likely to be much before a quarter to one.

FIFTEEN

As one grows older one is always expecting to stop enjoying Christmas or at least I am, and when Andrew and Rory burst into my bedroom at six o'clock on Christmas morning and wanted to show me what they'd had in their stockings, I cursed disagreeably, put my head under the bed-clothes and thought that the moment had come. However, when at half past seven they reappeared, this time with Cathy and Penny, things seemed brighter and when my stocking was handed to me I managed to unpack it in a suitably interested manner.

There were the usual things to eat, sweets, chocolate and a tangerine in the toe and the more exciting objects: a Penguin book on sailing, a pair of riding gloves, a film for my camera, a useful diary and a ballpoint pen. The others inspected my things and then produced their own; everyone had a book or two and the girls had collapsible hoof picks and dashing scarves. Rory's joy was a whistle which he blew piercingly and they spread on my bed their usual vast quantities of farm animals, Indians and Dinky cars.

When we had looked at everything, Andrew offered

Edinburgh rock, which we refused with horror except
for Rory who announced that he'd eaten a tangerine, a
Mars bar, two Kit Kats, fourteen Maltesers and half a
stick of barley sugar since six o'clock. When we'd told
him what a hog he was Cathy reminded us that it was
traditional to take the parents tea in bed at Christmas
and departed to make it, and I threw everyone out of my
room and dressed. Then I went downstairs and began to
ignite fires. The Old Kitchen fire is quite exciting to
light; it blazes up splendidly and when it is going you lay
a huge log from hob to hob. Then when the middle burns
through, you kick the two ends into the fire. The logs
were cherry and apple wood and soon a marvellous
smell pervaded the house.

My hands were better, so I did them up in sticking
plaster and when the girls appeared offered myself as a
milker. As we drank tea we decided that Penny and I
should milk and Cathy be in charge of breakfast, and
attiring myself in Dad's oilskin – it was raining again –
I instructed Andrew to look after the fires. We took
carrots for the ponies as well as their usual breakfasts
and since it was Christmas I controlled myself and didn't
remark on the dismal state of the corn-bin. The weather
was very lacking in Christmas spirit; rain fell steadily
and a huge bank of black storm-clouds glowered from
the south east. Carmen too was behaving in an un-
Christmassy way; her angry moos reached us as we
climbed Sutton's Hill. They pointed out that we were
over half an hour late.

In our family we open Christmas presents im-
mediately after breakfast. They are all arranged on
chairs in the sitting-room, one chair for each person and
we all charge in armed with knives and scissors and fall

upon them like vultures or starving wolves. Rory tears
his open without a glance at the label and so fast that it
needs both parents to make a list of who has sent him
what.

My presents were splendid. A proper sailing smock in
Breton red canvas with a lace-up front, from the
parents. A yellow tie decorated with foxes' masks from
Andrew and Penny, a photograph album from Rory and
from Cathy a book by my favourite author, who writes
novels about life at sea. There was a tremendously tough
sweater from Mum, who'd apparently knitted us each
one, navy blue for the boys and sapphire blue for the
girls. Then there were book tokens and books from
aunts and another tie, rather a subdued one, from a god-
mother, money from Grandfather, and sheepskin gloves
and a very nice riding whip from Grandmother. When
they were all open and strewn around me, I collapsed
with exhaustion and watched the parents, who, having
dealt with Rory's presents, were about to start on their
own.

Mum gave cries of delight over the Italian jug, they
sounded fairly genuine, and Dad seemed pleased with
the torch. Mummy, who has four sisters, had a lot of
feminine presents and Dad had given her a very
glamorous quilted dressing-gown, blue with large pink
roses.

"Oh, John, how lovely, but you shouldn't; it must
have cost the earth," she said.

But Dad answered that it was polyester, highly
practical and meant for everyday wear. When everything was unpacked we tried on our new clothes. Dad
put on his waistcoat and a pair of sheepskin gloves and a
scarf and stuck a white handkerchief with J on it that

Rory had given him in his breast pocket. Rory wore his new sweater, forced a knitted sailing cap an aunt had sent him over a space helmet and hung himself about with all the guns he'd been given.

Mum put on a pullover affair she called a golfer, a silk scarf and her new dressing-gown. She refused to wear a slip, three pairs of stockings and a pair of collapsible bedroom slippers, which were scarlet and clashed horribly with the dressing gown. Andrew wore two sweaters, two ties, a space helmet and what he called his best present, a watch from the parents. The girls looked extremely peculiar as they were wearing tough pull-overs with necklaces, bracelets, scarves and fur gloves, and I was in some difficulty as I had to exhibit my foxes' masks tie (which privately I thought rather young for me) from under my sailing smock.

When we'd all inspected each other's presents, Rory had made sure that everyone liked what he'd given them, when Mum had put the Italian jug in a place of honour and Dad had drawn the curtains and tried out the torch, we moved our possessions through to the Old Kitchen. We threw more logs on the fire and stood about gloating. Then we helped Andrew sort out the vast number of things his rich godfather had sent for the electric train; there was a second engine, a restaurant car and coaches, a tunnel, signal gantry and miles of track as well as the things we'd given him. Dad appeared, took one look and said we needed another table and I helped him fetch an elderly, cobwebby wooden kitchen table from the boothole where the coal lives, to save carrying it up from the cellar. We knocked off the worst of the cobwebs, found four pieces of wood to bring it up to the height of the other table and soon the railway was twice as large and there were so many signals, points and level crossings that Andrew needed a large staff to operate them all. At twelve o'clock the parents, wearing only suitable Christmas presents, departed to have a quick drink with some neighbours and we ate apples, gave Storm her presents – a marrow bone and a chocolate Father Christmas – and acted as Andrew's staff. Cathy and I were getting rather bored and had just announced that we were going to strike over our wage claim when the door opened and Nick came in; his arms were full of parcels.

"Hello," he said, and "Happy Christmas."

"Happy Christmas," we answered, looking at him with horror, for the parcels bore a ghastly resemblance to presents, and we hadn't one for him. And then there was Penny, her face had turned scarlet and from the look on it I couldn't decide whether she was going to speak, cut him or rush from the room in floods of tears.

Nick was obviously as embarrassed as we were; he stood by the door clutching his parcels and there was a hangdog look on his white face.

"Come and see the railway," I said hastily. "Andrew's godfather has sent him absolutely stacks more stuff. Have an apple?" I added as Nick deposited his parcels in a chair. Then the others came to life and began to offer sweets.

"Have some Edinburgh rock, Nick? It's excellent."

"Have a chocolate?"

"Have a Malteser?" Nick accepted an assortment of food and watched while Andrew despatched a train on the new circuit. Cathy and I nearly derailed it when we started discussing our wage claim instead of changing the points and Penny staged a fatal accident in which the woman in charge of the level-crossing gates wandered across the track in a fit of absentmindedness and was reduced to strawberry jam. Then Colonel Cleggs-Wighorn, who is one of my characters and a great stickler for punctuality, made a fearful scene at the next station because the train was two and a half minutes late. By the time Colonel Cleggs-Wighorn had been calmed by the station master – Andrew – and we'd found some farmyard men with shovels to clear up the mess on the level crossing we were all giggling helplessly and Penny was speaking to Nick. Then Nick said he'd only come for a sec and must go and that he'd brought us some presents.

"Oh Nick, you shouldn't." Cathy sounded exactly like Mum. And Rory announced bluntly, "We haven't got anything for you."

"That's all right," Nick answered, "I didn't expect you to. I mean you've been letting me ride your ponies and all that sort of thing." He handed the presents round hastily and began to back towards the door. Rory got his open first and with cries of "Great," and "Thanks, Nick" exhibited a battery-powered toy car. "Excellent," said Andrew brandishing a riding whip, and I said, "Thanks *awfully*, Nick," when I opened mine. It was a yachtsman's knife such as can only be bought from smart sailing shops in London. Cathy had a very superior fountain pen and Penny a large book on schooling horses. "Oh Nick," we said, "They're lovely, but you must have spent the earth." However Nick looked quite happy now that his presents had been such a success and when Cathy opened a box of liqueur chocolates a school friend had sent her we all began to giggle again. We ate each other's health in them and though they weren't real ones Rory and Andrew promptly announced that they were drunk and lurched about the room. Then I made Nick try on my smock and took him out to the hall to look at himself and when we came back the girls had evidently been plotting; they'd filled Cathy's pen and they asked Nick to use it and write "To Penny from Nick" in Penny's book. When he'd done that Nick looked at his watch and said that he simply must go, so we let him out of the side door and watched him as he tore down the lane. "Probably," I said, "his friends or relations, or whatever they are, are having their Christmas dinner at lunchtime and he's been told not to be late."

"Poor Nick," sighed Cathy, "I do wish we'd got him a present." But it was too late, the moment had passed.

SIXTEEN

This year, as Rory was considered old enough to stay up, we were having our Christmas dinner in the evening so we lunched off ham and baked potatoes and ice-cream, and afterwards the parents looked apprehensively at the torrents of rain, which still fell unceasingly, and funked the traditional Christmas walk. I was glad because I'd been seized with a sudden horror that Dad would decide to walk up to the Firs; but then he made other complications by saying that the ponies had better sleep at home as that would save us getting wet and they'd be dry in the morning. So, later on, when the others were bedding down the ponies for the night, Cathy and I simply tore to the Firs to milk and put Shamrock in. And all the way there and most of the way back – it's not so bad downhill – I was wishing that we'd already found Carmen a good country home.

At tea there was Christmas cake and only Rory was rash enough to eat more than once slice. Mum was wearing her slightly frenzied-looking expression and she kept leaping to her feet and darting into the kitchen to look at the turkey or see if the pudding had stopped boiling, but everything seemed to be all right. Then

Andrew remembered that it was traditional to play acting games and he nagged at Dad until we were all dragged into the sitting-room and made to play Adverbs which was very exhausting and cruelty to Cathy and me who only wanted to sit quietly and rest in a middle-aged manner after all the strenuous exercise we'd taken running to and from the Firs.

The dinner was delicious. Dad said that the turkey wasn't up to Charnworth standards, but no one else could taste any difference and, to Mum's surprise, the pudding emerged whole. Andrew got the sixpence and I had a thimble which pleased everybody. We pulled crackers and wore paper hats and read out riddles and mottoes like everyone else does at Christmas, and those of us who had any room left ate orange and lemon slices or dates or nuts, Rory was the first person to weaken and he went off to bed quite willingly for once. Mum announced that the washing-up could wait till morning, so we all moved into the sitting-room and played records until the hunting people said that they'd better go to bed as they had to get up early and I decided I might as well go too.

It rained all night. And on Boxing Day the rain was still falling from a stormy sky and the wind had grown stronger. Rory was asleep when the rest of us got up and as he wasn't hunting and he isn't much use we left him in bed. I went up to the Firs alone. Both Cathy and Penny offered to come with me but I had refused on the grounds that they had to groom their hunters and fetch Harlequin. Despite this, I felt cross, sleepy and very much the martyr as I climbed Sutton's Hill in the rain. Luckily I was home again by the time Mum appeared otherwise there might have been a spate of awkward questions to answer. As it was she thought I'd been feeding the bantams and helping my sisters. She was cooking breakfast and making sandwiches, so I started work on the monstrous pile of dirty dishes. I washed them gloomily, wishing that I was hunting and feeling more and more a martyr with every moment. At intervals Mum told me what an angel I was, which was very irritating as it spoiled my martyrdom. The hunting people came in, gobbled some breakfast and dashed out again. Rory and I had breakfast together and Mum said she'd wait for Dad. When Cathy and Penny came in to change Penny was in a state; she announced angrily that Harlequin was absolutely filthy and a disgrace. Mum told her that long-coated ponies weren't expected to look smart, but she refused to be calmed and stumped upstairs muttering furiously.

"Douglas, darling, go and look and see if he is too awful," said Mum persuasively so, swearing and cursing, I had to make a dash through the rain to the stable. I must say Harlequin did look a bit odd. His white parts were damp and dun-coloured and his mane, which had stood up stiffly for so long, had started to lie down; it had parted in the middle and stuck out sideways, looking like two rather peculiar brushes. Short of hogging his mane and washing the rest of him there didn't seem much I could do, besides, I thought, remembering the rain, they would all look like drowned rats by the time they'd hacked the eight miles to Spayborne. Merlin was looking dry, handsome and excited and in Jess's loose box I found Andrew solemnly picking out her hoofs.

"For heaven's sake hurry up," I said. "It's a quarter to ten and the girls are practically dressed."

"Oh dear, I haven't *nearly* finished. Her tail's all tangled and her white sock's not white," wailed Andrew in desperate tones. "Oh go and change! I'll finish her," I said wearily. "Thanks awfully." He brightened up at once and as he went out of the loose box he asked, "Which of my new ties do you think I should wear? Horses' heads or cowboys?"

"Whichever you like least," I answered, starting on Jess. "Because it'll be ruined by the time you get to Spayborne."

"Oh, perhaps I'd better wear an old one then," said Andrew in doubtful and disappointed tones. He stood in an agony of indecision. "If you don't hurry up you won't get there at all." I reminded him. "It's now ten minutes to ten." He ran then and as he went into the house he was greeted by angry shrieks from the girls. Presently they emerged, looking very clean and polished, and they buttoned their macintoshes indignantly as the rain came down harder than ever. I decided Jess would have to do and saddled and bridled her and then – as Cathy was beginning to fuss and Penny to fume – I went indoors to hurry Andrew. Mum was already on the job and as Andrew dashed past me into the kitchen passage, dropping money, sandwiches and his new riding whip in his haste, she pursued him with the belt of Rory's macintosh which she was trying to attach to his.

At last we got them off and then we collapsed in chairs round the kitchen table while Mum tried to make up her mind what we were having for lunch. When that was settled we had elevenses to revive us before tidying up the bits that showed under macintoshes and departing for the meet. We took the little car and Storm came and sat between Rory and me in the back. The rain still fell in torrents at times the windscreen wipers were overwhelmed and Dad had to slow right down. "Oh, what a shame," Mum kept saying, and "They'll be soaked through," and "We'd better tell them to start home at two." "Three," said Dad, "don't forget the meet's an hour later today." And, "If it's still raining like this I'm not going to try to follow." "No," agreed Mum, "there's no point; we shouldn't see a thing."

Rory began to moan, but Dad was looking for somewhere to park so he was ignored. Spayborne was choc-a-bloc with cars and trailers and people despite the weather. All the local farmworkers and their wives seemed to have come and the townspeople were there huddled under umbrellas, but macintoshed and capped or felt-hatted types predominated and they called to each other cheerfully or stood in groups discussing the weather and beef prices and whether hounds would find. Dad is well known in this part of the world and people kept calling "Good morning" to him, but it soon became obvious that he didn't want to be drawn into conversation. By the time we reached hounds, who waited disconsolately by the Christmas tree outside the Town Hall, Dad had said that the weather was terrible and the night had been so rough all the foxes would be underground, at least a dozen times as he hurried away from his friends and acquaintances.

A few smart people hunt with the Spay Vale Foxhounds. I saw four top-hatted men, two really posh women, but otherwise the field is nearly all farmers. Enormously fat farmers on weight carriers, tall thin farmers on blood weeds, farmers' sons on wild-eyed youngsters. They all wore riding hats and black coats that had seen better days and the farmers' sons mostly wore boots that had belonged to someone else and didn't quite fit. I saw several people I knew, but somehow I'd got infected by Dad's mood and I fled from them and when Cathy, Penny and Andrew arrived, Rory and I went over to talk to them. The parents had been caught by the Hunt Secretary who was plying them with cherry brandy and inquiring whether Mr. Smithson was likely to be more helpful to the hunt than the Charnworths: Lord Charnworth had been too much of a shooting man to please. As soon as the parents could escape they joined us and we all talked together. Cathy said her mac sleeves were leaking and she had trickles of water running down her arms and Andrew announced that he was starving and started on his sandwiches. Rory escaped from Mum and dived right into the middle of the pack, whereupon he was nearly knocked over by a rush of maternally minded hounds who all wanted to put their paws on his shoulders and lick his face. I, of course, was sent to retrieve him. After nearly twenty minutes in the unabating rain we were all glad when the cherry-brandy drinkers mounted and hounds moved off. As we waved good-bye to the hunting Conways and turned towards the car a tall man with a lined face and a grey moustache, who was wearing a macintosh and cap, stopped Dad. "Morning, Conway," he said, "How are you? Keeping fit I hope."

"Yes thanks, Colonel," answered Dad, edging away.

The Colonel pursued us. "How are you getting on with this chap Smithson?" he asked.

"Not too badly; we have our ups and downs of course," Dad answered evenly.

"More downs than ups, eh? From what I've been hearing anyway," laughed the Colonel.

"I wouldn't say that," Dad answered coldly, hurrying down the street.

The Colonel wasn't to be shaken off. He hurried too. "Must be a bit of a change for you though," he said sympathetically. "No joke working for one of these rich Jew boys when you've been used to a man like Charnworth."

Dad looked furious. "What's being a Jew got to do with it?" he demanded.

The Colonel looked surprised. He laughed uneasily. "Well, I mean there's a whale of a difference between working for a man like Charnworth – born and bred to it – and one of these get-rich-quick Jew boys."

"Nonsense," Dad roared at him. "I don't care if a man's a Lord or a Jew or if he's black; as long as he's a good employer and fond of the land I'll work for him."

"So you're getting on all right with this Smithson feller," said the Colonel. "Well, I'm glad to hear it, Conway, very glad indeed."

Dad lost his temper. "If you really want to know, I'm not getting on with him at all," he roared, "but when I leave it'll have absolutely nothing to do with Mr. Smithson's religion." And having reached the car he got in and banged the door shut. We piled in hastily, and the Colonel looking puzzled and rather alarmed took himself off.

"Wretched old Fascist," muttered Dad. "His sort make me see red."

"I wonder if he is?" said Mum.

"If who's what?" asked Dad irritably.

"If Mr. Smithson is a *Jew*; he may be."

Dad beat the steering wheel with both hands. "I don't know and I don't care," he answered vehemently.

"What difference does it make to us?"

"None at all," answered Mum. "I was just wondering." Dad drove off, wrenching at the gears and swearing. When he was clear of the scrum of cars and out of Spayborne, he turned to Mum and said, "You know, it's never occurred to me before, but supposing Smithson thinks I'm like that? He probably thinks I regret Lord Charnworth because he was a lord and not because I liked him. He may even suspect *me* of muttering about get-rich-quick Jew boys; he probably thinks that's why I don't take to him."

Dad had evidently forgotten us, so I gave Rory, who'd begun to wriggle, a look which said "keep quiet or else—"

"I've never discovered why you don't like him," said Mum.

"Oh, I don't know. It isn't that I *dislike* him exactly," Dad spoke thoughtfully. "But I've always got the feeling that he suspects me of making off with the money or at least feathering my nest and that he's got Ross in on the principle of setting a land agent to catch a land agent. Lord Charnworth wasn't intelligent and he could be as obstinate as the devil but he had a marvellous way of putting people at their ease, but this chap either hasn't got it or he doesn't want people at their ease. And then I used to be the go-ahead one. I used to suggest modernisations and improvements to Lord Charnworth and he acted as a brake. Now the position's reversed, Mr. Smithson and Ross suggest changes and crack-brained schemes all day long and I'm forced to behave like a die-hard grandfather and turn them all down. It makes me feel I'm old and out of date."

"That's nonsense," said Mum. "You're just level-headed. And look at the job you had persuading Lord Charnworth to install the grain dryer and what a success it's been."

Dad had caught sight of us in the driving mirror and he hastily shook off his gloom. "You boys are very quiet at the back," he said in hearty tones. "What's the matter? Still sleeping off Christmas?"

It rained all afternoon. I'd quite stopped envying the hunting Conways and I sat snugly in the Old Kitchen writing thank-you letters. I made masses of mistakes because my mind would wander to the dismal problems of what we were to do if we left Charnworth, of whether Carmen and Shamrock would ever find good country homes and the less serious but more immediate one of what reason I could give for disappearing to the Firs to milk; Dad had already announced that the ponies were to be stabled. I had only two letters left to write when the door opened and Nick slid in. "Hullo," he said, and "I've done mine; but perhaps I don't have as many to write as you do," he added rather wistfully.

"We've dozens of aunts and things," I admitted. "They're mostly on Mum's side and being Scottish they've a clan instinct; they hang together, and you're expected to be cousinly with your third cousins twice removed and that sort of thing."

"It must be nice," said Nick.

"It's a bore sometimes," I told him. "Do you want to come and milk?" I asked sticking down envelopes. "You needn't," I added, looking out at the murky afternoon. "I shall think you're mad if you do."

Nick said he'd come so I went through to borrow Dad's oilskin and announced that I was going for a walk with Nick for the sake of my liver. Rory was standing on

the upstairs landing dropping his new parachutist over
the banisters and watching him descend to the hall; he'd
been doing it all afternoon. When he heard me telling
Mum that Nick and I were going for a walk he said he
was coming too. "No you're not," said Mum, who'd
seen by my face that I didn't want him; "it's too wet and
they'll want to hurry. Take Storm, Douglas," she called
to me as I fled from Rory's fury. Someone let Storm out
of the sitting-room and I explained to Nick that the
feeds were up at the Firs, I'd taken a double lot up before
breakfast.

It was hard work walking up Sutton's Hill. We
seemed to be blown back two steps for every one we
took forward and the rain, which lashed one's face, was
hard as hail. Along the road Storm walked obediently at
heel and Nick began to wish he had a dog. He asked if
Storm had had any puppies. I explained that we meant to
breed from her but, like everything else it had been put
off when Lord Charnworth died and that we wanted
some more dogs ourselves, because Storm is so devoted
to Dad she can't count as a family dog.

We milked and Carmen was just as beastly to Nick as
she had been to us when we first had her. She put a hind
leg in the bucket three times and kicked him and the
milking stool and the bucket over twice, but whenever I
took over she behaved. Nick swore that Shamrock was
miles fatter, but I didn't altogether trust his judgement.
And anyway, I was overcome by gloom, having rashly
calculated the number of hay bales left; so I only
answered that the sooner we found both her and
Carmen homes the better and we were advertising them
next week. As we walked home through the wet dusk
we heard hoofs from behind and soon the hunting Con-

ways caught up with us. We told them that officially we
were walking for the good of our livers and asked what
sort of day they'd had.

"Excellent," said Andrew enthusiastically. "We
galloped for miles and miles and jumped at least four
things and Jess was terribly good."

The girls were less enthusiastic. Penny explained that
most of the galloping had been when the field master
thought he'd lost hounds and had galloped round the
countryside looking for them, only to find that they had
never left the original wood. And Cathy said that the
jumps hadn't been very exciting: a ditch, two lots of slip
rails and a broken-down hedge. In fact it had been a
blank day but, they said, "Quite fun." When we
reached the end of our lane Penny said she was going to
bring Harlequin home for a feed and turn him out afterwards and I tried to persuade Nick to come to tea
because, apart from anything else, I'd remembered that
we owed him money. But he shied away at the very
thought and said he couldn't possibly; he was expected
back, in fact he was already late, and that we could pay
him next time he came. So we said good night and left
him there alone, a very forlorn-looking figure in the
dark and the rain.

SEVENTEEN

It was still raining on Sunday and even Dad, who doesn't usually grumble about the weather, began to complain.

"Three days' holiday and they're all wet," he said. "The floods'll be out too; it was pretty wet down at Holmford on Christmas Eve, I should think the village is awash by now."

The ponies were still being cosseted and waiting in the stable for the rain to stop and Cathy and I sneaked off to milk while the others mucked out. The parents were going out to lunch with the Conway grandparents, who have retired to a cottage in a seaside village about thirty miles from Charnworth. We couldn't all go because the cottage is tiny, and Grandfather, who'd been ill, wouldn't want a noise, but the parents said they'd take Rory and Storm. Mum fussed rather over what the rest of us would eat for lunch, but we settled on ham omelettes and fried Christmas pudding and ignored her threats of duodenal ulcers and scurvy through eating too much fried food and not enough vegetables.

When we'd seen them off, we lit the Old Kitchen fire, there were still masses of wood left, and got down to letter writing. I soon finished mine and then I read.

Our lunch was splendid and afterwards we all felt much too full and had to collapse into chairs to digest. But about two o'clock the rain stopped and the sky, though still grey, was lighter. We decided that we'd better take the ponies back while the going was good and we'd take up a brush to groom Shamrock and a pitchfork to muck out her stable and that Carmen would just have to put up with being milked early.

When we'd collected everything we set off, Andrew and I on the ponies and the girls carrying the pitchfork and dandy brush. As we neared the bridge we could see that the floods were well and truly out. Bridge Meadow and Brook Meadow were stretches of water indistinguishable from the river and so was Sutton's Marsh on the other bank. Only the fact that the road is raised saved it from being under water and already the flood in Bridge Meadow lapped hungrily at the bank. Below the bridge the flood narrowed but it still filled the whole stretch between the foot of Charnworth Down and the rising ground on which Nutsford stands and it was flowing fast. A swirling torrent of dun-coloured water pouring down towards the sea and carrying with it a mass of branches, logs and uprooted reeds.

"It's pretty impressive, isn't it?" Andrew said.

"So long as it doesn't flood the road and cut us off from the Firs; I can just hear Carmen's angry moos," I remarked. Penny was hanging over the parapet. "It's right up to the top of the arches," she told us.

"Am I mad?" asked Cathy, who was staring across the fields. "Or are there some animals out on the meads?" We all swung round hastily to look. "There's something there," I agreed. And Penny said, "It looks like cows to me."

"It can't be," we said, looking at each other. "They never put cows on the meads in winter." Then we looked again and the things were still there.

"I suppose we'd better go round and see," I said with reluctance.

"What, through all that water?" asked Andrew apprehensively.

"No, you know the way; down by the Green Lane from the village," Cathy told him. And Penny added, "If we go through the field by the rickyard we can get into the Green Lane half-way down." The ponies were furious when we turned back towards the village, they dawdled and sulked.

We didn't hurry. I thought the objects were probably thorn bushes and we'd just never noticed them before, and Cathy produced a theory that seeing cows where there weren't any was an early symptom of scurvy. We all looked about to see if we could see strange objects elsewhere, but the only other cows we saw were in the home farm fields and they looked real enough. At the rickyard Andrew and I gave our mounts to the girls and we left the pitchfork and brush by the gate to collect on our way back. "I hope the F.W. doesn't appear," said Andrew nervously as we crossed Parson's Close. On the other side of the field Andrew and I tugged open a reluctant gate which led into the Green Lane. The lane was squelchy and waterlogged in places and Penny, who was in the lead, soon called out that she could see the hoofprints of cattle. We all began to hurry then. "I just don't see how they could have got there," I protested. "The meads are *never* grazed in winter. Everyone knows that the river can rise ten feet in a couple of hours." We hurried on between the tall thorn hedges until the lane

ended at the five-barred gate into Ash Mead. Andrew
and I tugged it open and we left it open behind us as we
went out on to the mead. About half Ash Mead was
under water, the lower half lying nearest to the river,
and there were no cows to be seen. We looked right-
handed to Long Mead and saw them at once. Eight of the
Charnworth Jersey heifers marooned on a grassy island,
perilously close to the rising river. We hurried across
Ash Mead, sloshing through ankle-deep water to the
gate between the meads. Not all of Long Meadow was
flooded but the heifers had chosen the wrong piece of
high ground. Not only was it near the river but a small
stream flowed across that part of the field carrying
water from a spring to join the Spay. In the summer the
stream was no more than a wet ditch, full of rushes and
kingcups, but now the Spay was flowing back along it;
the ditch and the bridge which crossed it and the river
bank had all disappeared under a sheet of water, and the
stupid little cows were cut off. We had to walk carefully
to avoid shipping bootfuls and soon Andrew cursed.
"It's over the top of my boots," he said. "Well, go back
a bit and wait," I told him, "there's no point in getting
wetter than we need." Jess too was beginning to fuss.
"Somewhere between us and them is that ditch," I said.
"What we want is the hump bridge, isn't it somewhere
near the thorn bush?"

"Yes, it's to the right of the bush," answered Cathy.

"Are you sure?" I asked. "I don't want to fall in if I
can help it."

"Fairly sure," answered Cathy.

And Penny added, "Yes, of course it is."

I advanced a bit farther, evidently into a hollow, and
got two good bootfuls of water. It wasn't too badly cold,

but I cursed and stepped back. "Lend me Merlin a sec," I said to Penny. "If I can ride him over the bridge I may be able to drive them back."

"Why can't I go?" asked Penny.

Cathy began to object at once. "No, Penny, you're not to," she said, and I backed her up. Cathy and I are both adequate swimmers, but Penny isn't; it's the one thing she's not much good at. "If we miss the bridge we'll be in the ditch," I told her, "and it's quite deep. There must be at least five feet of water and if anyone's going to fall in. I'm the tallest. Ride back a bit before you dismount or it'll be over your boots."

Penny dismounted with a splash and legged me up and, wishing I had a bridle instead of just a halter, I urged Merlin forward and steered him towards the thorn bush and, I hoped, the bridge. I tried to remember the bridge from summer rides. It was really just an outsize drainpipe covered with earth and stone and topped with turf, about four feet wide, I thought; trying to estimate how far I could venture from the thorn bush. Merlin stumbled a little when he stepped into the hollow where I got my bootfuls and then he went on bravely and we seemed to be on the bridge. Less and less of his legs disappeared into the water as we advanced up the hump. I looked ahead at the heifers, huddled together on their island, and tried to think of a way to drive them across. Then Merlin stumbled, one of his feet must have missed the side of the bridge, he lost his balance and we both fell sideways. I clawed helplessly at the air and then with a tremendous splash we hit the water. Having no stirrups in which to become entangled I was thrown clear, and came up gasping to find myself in shoulder-deep water. Merlin was threshing about beside me; I tried to grab his halter rope but was driven back by his flailing hoofs. Mud and water churned as he fought frantically for a foothold. He'll break his back, I thought desperately. But suddenly he got a purchase on the side of the ditch and Cathy grabbed his halter rope from above, then she pulled and I yelled and waved my arms to encourage him to make a last effort, and with a lurch and a heave he struggled out. I sloshed around trying to get out but I couldn't get a foothold either until Penny appeared and gave me a hand. Merlin was upset. He stood trembling with hanging head and heaving sides.

"That's hopeless," said Cathy. "You can't possibly try that again. Merlin'll break a leg or you'll get squashed or something."

"Well, I'm so wet now I can just wade through it," I answered. "I was only trying to keep dry and I thought he might round the heifers up. If everyone gives me their mac belts it will help, but we're going to need halters and a rope to get them across the bridge. Penny and Andrew had better ride for help. I stripped off Dad's oilskin which was now a hindrance. "Chuck this down by the gate," I said to Penny, "and gallop to Home Farm. Collect halters and a rope and tell Bill Martin and anyone else you see what's happened."

EIGHTEEN

Penny and Andrew splashed away through the flood water and as soon as they were out of it they really galloped. We watched them until they disappeared into the green lane and then we turned back to the heifers. Their island had shrunk. Cathy handed me a mac belt and we made for the bridge. "Let me go first," I said, "because I'm so wet I don't mind if I do fall in again." "Aren't you icy?" asked Cathy. "No, the water isn't as cold as all that," I answered, "and I've warmed up what's inside my clothes. I feel rather as though I was wearing nice warm soup next to the skin."

It was less nerve-racking crossing the bridge on one's own feet; one could feel for land before taking each step. On the far side of the bridge there was another hollow and the water was knee deep, but after that it became progressively shallower until we stepped on to the heifers' waterlogged, but still green island. They looked at us hopefully and mooed plaintively. We caught two of them and buckled macintosh belts round their necks and led them towards the bridge. They followed willingly enough until we reached the hollow where the water became knee deep; there they jibbed. At first we were patient, we spoke soothing words and patted and stroked them. Then we tried shouting and threats, but they stood, their brown eyes bulging with fright and refused to move. "I'll let mine go," I said after several frustrating minutes, "and try shoving yours from behind." I shoved Cathy's heifer and I beat it over the rump with a macintosh belt. I tried yelling and waving my arms. And Cathy tried tugging and encouraging words, but the wretched cow refused to budge. We were becoming desperate when we saw a figure running across the field towards us, splashing through the floor water. "It's Nick," observed Cathy. I was longing for Bill Martin or George White or someone who understood heifers better than I did and would take charge, but still, Nick was an extra person to pull or push.

He was out of breath. "Penny sent me," he gasped. Cathy handed him the leading macintosh belt; she'd buckled two together. "Pull for all you're worth," she said, "and mind you don't get trampled on." Then she came and joined me behind the heifer. I explained to Nick about the bridge and the deep ditch on either side and then we tried to get the heifer across; we pushed and shoved and pulled, but without effect; the heifer braced her forelegs and resisted.

"It's maddening," said Cathy breathlessly, "because she isn't very big; we ought to be able to move her."

"I think we could if we had a halter," I answered. "I wish Penny would hurry up." Then I saw a large and intimidating-looking stick floating near and I sloshed along to get it. It seemed rather mean to use it on the heifer, but meaner still, I thought, to leave her to be swept away or to starve. "Look out," I called to the others and then I rushed at the heifer yelling and brandishing my stick in a frenzied manner. I brought it down with a crack on her rump and she simply leapt forward, but she missed her footing on the bridge and went straight into the ditch. Nick overbalanced and landed in a sitting position in the flood. The poor little cow disappeared entirely and for an awful moment I thought she was going to drown; but then her soaking, terrified face appeared and she scrabbled for a foothold on the bank. I made for the ditch to push her from behind, but somehow she managed by herself and emerged dripping and shaken. Cathy patted and calmed her and then led her through the water to Ash Mead to turn her loose. Nick and I took the third mac belt and went back for another cow. The water was deeper and the island had all but gone. I led the heifer and Nick chivvied from behind, but she came willingly enough until we reached the patch of deep water and there, like the first one, she jibbed. Cathy had come back. "Do be careful," she said. "They could drown in the ditch, or break a leg." "Yes, I know," I answered, "I'll try not to produce such startling results again." I was prodding the water with my stick trying to find the two edges of the bridge. When I'd found them we pointed the heifer bang at the middle of the bridge and Cathy buckled all three mac belts together so that she could stand back to pull. Then Nick pushed and I tried a series of gentle taps. Eventually this heifer jumped forward too, but she landed squarely in the middle of the bridge and Cathy pulled her across and let her go; whereupon she hurried mooing to join the first one by the Ash Mead gate.

Then we saw Penny coming. She was galloping through a cloud of spray, but when she slowed up and the spray subsided we could see she carried halters and a rope. "Bill Martin's not there," she told us breathlessly, "he's got the day off. George and Bert were milking and they're coming as soon as they can and I sent Andrew home to see if Dad was back and to leave a note if he wasn't. I didn't see anyone else except Nick, oh and Mrs. Browne. I told her to tell any of the men she saw." "Well, these are fine," I said, taking the halters and rope from her. "We can probably get them across ourselves now. You stay there, Penny, and we'll chuck you the end of the rope to pull."

There were three halters and Cathy, Nick and I decided to bring two heifers to the bridge and see if one would follow the other over. The island had completely disappeared and the water was beginning to swirl in an ominous way. All across the field you could see it gathering speed and it felt strong and purposeful as it swirled against my boots. With the disappearance of the heifers' island the river and the field had become one, a great dun-coloured sea and only a very occasional bush or tree indicated the river bank. We caught two more heifers. Now they had no island they were beginning to scatter; they lowed apprehensively. The sky had grown darker, the wind stronger, the atmosphere was suddenly frightening and I found myself looking across to Ash Mead to make sure our way of escape hadn't been cut off. The others had been awed by the atmosphere too. We didn't speak, but we became desperate in our haste. And as we hurried the heifers towards the bridge, a few great raindrops fell from the angry sky. The halters gave us much more control and, by using the rope as well, the girls were able to stand in comparatively shallow water to pull instead of trying to keep their footing on the bridge. I tapped with the intimidating stick and Nick held the other heifer near in the hope that she would decide to follow. She didn't, and when the first one was safely across we had to put the rope on the second; but she made less fuss and soon she was over too. While the girls sent them on their way towards Ash Mead, Nick and I hurried to fetch another. The water was over our boots now almost everywhere. Walking was becoming more and more difficult. We hurried the heifer to the bridge and tied the rope on, but this one was a devil; she wouldn't go. Then we saw Andrew riding back and Penny called to him to take Merlin so that she would have two hands with which to pull. We pushed and shoved and tugged and yelled and finally I walloped, which resulted in another leap forward, but the girls managed to keep the rope taut and the heifer safely on the bridge, and in a moment she was over.

There were only three left. It was just as well, I thought, judging by the rate at which the water was rising. We hurried back for number six. She was less obstinate and we soon got her across. As we floundered after number seven in water that was rapidly becoming waist deep, I saw the Land Rover in Ash Mead. "Reinforcements," I shouted to Nick. But he didn't seem to hear. His face stayed white and strained. Our technique was improving or else the heifers becoming more apprehensive of what was behind them than of what lay ahead. Number seven crossed the bridge gladly and Nick and I set off in pursuit of the last one. She'd lost her nerve and floundered about recklessly, trying to find her way to shallower water. We caught her just as Dad reached the bridge and called out anxiously to know if we were all right. "Fine," I yelled back confidently, feeling very cheerful now that we had our last cow. But our heifer suddenly decided to drown where she was, She refused to move. Nick pulled and forgetting to be cautious I sloshed round behind to give her a shove. Suddenly the ground slithered from under me, I felt myself going down and down; murky waters closed over my head. I realised I was in the river and panicking. I fought wildly against the powerful current. I surfaced choking and found myself helpless. I was really frightened as I struggled against the current in an attempt to get back to Nick and was borne impotently away. I realised that my boots were heavy, my clothes waterlogged and I was already tired. I'm going to drown I thought, and I began to fight again frenziedly. It was no use, the volume of water was a thousand times stronger than I was and I was borne rapidly downstream.

Then someone's words of wisdom came into my mind. "Never fight a current," I'd been told. "Go with it, you can always get out farther down."

I stopped struggling. I looked ahead and used my energy to edge towards the bank as I was carried along. I saw a black alder, coned and catkinned; I would try to get out there, I thought, and I began to save energy for the effort. As I drew near I swam frantically towards the bank. But I couldn't quite make it, I felt myself being swept by. I stretched out a despairing hand and felt a submerged branch; I grabbed and hung on and it held. I pulled myself along it until I reached the tree and then I rested against its many stems in a tangle of driftwood and reeds. Dad appeared, white-faced and anxious and knee deep in water.

"Look out," I told him, "you're on the brink." He stretched out a hand to me and another to the people behind him so they made a human chain and they hauled until I found land under my feet. "Are you all right?" asked Dad.

"Yes, a bit waterlogged, that's all," I answered, which wasn't quite true; I felt awfully weak.

Mum said, "Oh, Douglas, you did give us a fright," in reproachful tones and I realised that she'd been part of the human chain.

"What about Nick? Has he got that heifer across?" I asked.

"Yes, Ogden and White have got her," answered another voice and I realised that the F.W. was there too. I'd come out right down the end of Long Mead and when I'd collected my wits we walked up the field to join the others, who were leading the eighth heifer back; we all met at the Ash Mead gate. "Are you all right, Douglas?" Cathy asked. "Yes, fine," I answered. And Andrew said, "Ugh, it looked awful." He shuddered. "I thought you were going to drown."

"What I can't understand," said Dad looking puzzled, "is how the heifers got there. They're supposed to be in the ten acre. Do you know anything about it, George?" George White looked embarrassed. "'Twas us brought them down," he said, "on Christmas Eve."

"You *brought* them down?" demanded Dad. "But why? You know we don't use the meads in the winter. Has everyone gone mad?"

"'Twas Bill who said to bring them," George White answered looking everywhere but at Dad. "He'd had 'is orders, 'e said, but whether it was from Mr. Smithson or Mr. Ross I couldn't quite make out."

Dad stood for a moment letting this sink in and then he turned on the F.W. and his face was ablaze with anger. "This is the last straw," he shouted. "This week's been quite unbearable; I've put up with pinpricks and downright rudeness, but I'm not going to stand for this. If Ross gives the orders he can have the job; I've finished." Dad had forgotten that he had an audience; Mum and all of us, George, Bert and Nick all staring at him in open-mouthed horror, but the F.W. was well aware of us. "Very well, Conway, if that's how you want it," he said in a quiet and angry voice, "but we'll discuss the details another time, the important thing now is to take these children home. Nicholas," he called. And Nick, white-faced and dripping wet, gave us a despairing look and followed him through the gate My teeth began to chatter with cold and misery, but my brain refused to contemplate what had happened. Dad asked the men if they could manage. And Mum said, "Come on, John, these children are soaking." "What about the ponies?" asked Dad, shepherding us towards the Land Rover. The thought of Carmen and Shamrock merely added to my misery, but Penny spoke up briskly. "Andrew and I'll take them," she said. "You're not wet, are you, Andrew?" she asked. "No, not a bit," he answered.

"All right then," said Dad, stooping to leg Penny up, "but hurry; we don't want you out in the dark and you don't feel as dry as all that. Come on in with the rest of you," he went on, letting down the back of the Land Rover.

"Why did Nick go off with the F.W.?" asked Rory as we drove slowly up Green Lane. Cathy and I didn't answer, we didn't know, but Dad said, "Nick? You mean that boy was your friend Nick?"

"Yes," we answered dismally.

"Well, his name's not de Veriac – it's Smithson. He's

the old man's nephew; I was introduced to him on Christmas Eve."

"But he can't be," wailed Rory and burst into a flood of tears. He cried and sobbed all the way home and I wished I was young enough to sob and cry, to kick and throw things as well, because that was what I felt like. But being too old I sat and shivered in silence. Storm fussed about trying to lick Cathy and me dry, and Dad spoke quietly to Mum, "I'm sorry to let you in for that, Fi," he said, "but I think it had to come."

"Yes, there's a limit to what one can put up with," she answered. "And you'll find something else."

We disembarked at the front door and saw Andrew's notice still pinned to it: *Some Hefers are out on the Meeds and we are rescuing them. Andrew.*

Mum said, "Hot baths, you two. Come on, don't stand there; you look frozen. You go first, Cathy, you're the quickest. Douglas, you can take off your clothes and put on your dressing-gown while you're waiting."

Dad said, "Whisky's the stuff. Hot whisky and lemon." He collected a bottle from the sitting-room and disappeared in the direction of the kitchen. Mum chivvied Cathy and me in and out of the bathroom, into dry clothes and downstairs into the Old Kitchen, where we found Dad had stirred the fire into a blaze. He produced hot drinks for everyone, even Rory, who hadn't got wet. "I've left Penny's and Andrew's in the saucepan," he said. Mine seemed to be mostly whisky. I began to feel hot and sleepy and more pleasantly numb. Presently Mum sent Dad to change and took Rory to the kitchen to help her with tea. Cathy and I were left, one on each side of the fire.

Cathy spoke first. "How could Nick?" she asked in a

shaky voice. "How could he tell us all those lies?"

"I suppose he just isn't the person we thought he was," I answered wearily. "I suppose he's just beastly through and through. He probably had a good laugh at the way we swallowed his stories." I sat and squirmed as I tortured myself by remembering the things we'd told him, the things he could have passed on. And then I said, "Oh hell, what does he matter compared with leaving Nutsford and Charnworth?"

"We shall have to tell Dad about Shamrock and Carmen," observed Cathy.

"Yes, but not yet," I answered irritably. "Give him time to get over this." Where would we be by the Easter holidays, I wondered. Not at Nutsford. We wouldn't be here to gallop on Charnworth Down on showery April mornings. Or to spend long, hot summer days swimming in the Spay. No Conways would help with the hay-making or watch the corn harvested, or pick the apples or climb the trees or milk the cows. Mr. Ross would have the house. The dear house in which we'd lived for eight long years. Rory had been born here, Andrew couldn't remember living anywhere else; I couldn't *imagine* living anywhere else. Misery pricked at my eyes and constricted my chest.

"I suppose Dad will get another job," said Cathy.

"Yes, I suppose so," I answered. But I knew that good jobs for land agents are few and far between; that this had been a plum job; and that when you have five children you daren't stay out of work for long, but take the first thing you're offered.

Penny and Andrew came in through the side door and told us that they'd managed Carmen and Shamrock. And Cathy told them about Nick. "We thought it must be something like that," said Andrew, "when we saw them go off together." And Penny said, "Tomorrow I'm going to burn his book."

Then Dad appeared with whisky and lemon for them and when they'd drunk it he sent them to change, ignoring their protests that they weren't the least wet, they'd dried out running home. Mum was calling "Tea". She'd boiled us all eggs and, though I wasn't a bit hungry, I did feel better when I'd been forced to devour an enormous tea. And afterwards the parents announced that they would "save" the sitting-room fire by sitting in the Old Kitchen with us and Dad and I carried in extra chairs.

We built up a huge fire and Mum produced chestnuts and put Penny and Andrew on to roasting them. They didn't seem very good at it and there were constant explosions. Then Dad, looking rather embarrassed and beating an apple log with a poker, gave us a lecture. He said that because we'd all been so happy at Nutsford it didn't mean that we couldn't be happy anywhere else. He said that it was the people in the family who made it, not the place where they lived and that wherever we went we would have each other and the ponies and Storm and that was a great deal more than most people have. "Leaving Nutsford isn't the end of the world," he said, "so don't let's go round behaving as though it is."

NINETEEN

Monday, the first working day after Christmas, was fine. The rain had stopped in the night and a pale sun shone mockingly as Cathy and I rode home on the ponies. The floods were still out; but today they reflected a placid sky and seagulls bobbing like ducks on a pond gave them a homely look. The darkness and drama of the day before had gone; I felt cheated and tired; I wanted the excitement of storms and tempests to buoy me up; to face leaving Nutsford in calm, cold blood was going to need a lot more courage. Cathy and I didn't talk much. We agreed that after breakfast we'd write an advertisement of Shamrock and Carmen, buy a postal order, and send it off and when we'd settled that, there didn't seem anything left to discuss.

We reached home just as Dad came in and we all went into breakfast together. Mum said, "You haven't been long, John," and he answered, "No, I only went as far as Home Farm." He ate a few mouthfuls of bacon and tomato and then he added, "I saw Bill." He made a rueful face. "The silly old fool," he said affectionately, "he hasn't half made a mess of things. On Christmas Eve someone told him I'd been given the push and apparently

it upset him. Then when Mr. Smithson and Ross turned
up with their usual strings of questions and wanted to
know why we fed so much hay to the heifers when there
was all that keep on the meads, he thought he'd let them
find out for themselves and simply said that it was my
orders. It seems that Ross sneered at me and said of
course I was the boss and everything I said was to be
taken as gospel. But I don't think anyone actually told
Bill to put the cattle out there; he'd just had enough. But
he goes on and on and round and round the point; you
know what he is when he's upset. I think myself that he
thought he'd spite Ross and he didn't realise the floods
would be as bad as they are. Apparently they haven't
been like this since '47.''

"What will happen then?" asked Mum.

"Oh, he'll have to go too," Dad answered. "You
couldn't really expect anyone to keep him after that.
Anyway he wants to go; but he's not a young man and all
his roots are here—" Dad sighed. "Oh well, it's a fine
day," he said. "Like to come round with me this
morning, Douglas?" ·

I wasn't sure whether he wanted to cheer me up or
whether I was being invited to cheer him, but I accepted
at once and about twenty minutes later, duffle-coated
and gum-booted, we set off in the Land Rover, with
Storm as usual in the back.

"We'll go to the sawmill first," said Dad, turning
towards Spayborne. We drove past the Firs and then
took the narrow little road which leads round the far
side of Charnworth Down and up to Forest Hill. No one
at the sawmill was working. The men all stood in a
group talking earnestly and I recognised some of the
forest workers, who'd evidently dropped in.

Dad made a rueful face and said, "Oh dear, doesn't news travel?" The head forester came across to the Land Rover, "Is it true this time, John?" he asked. "Yes, afraid so," Dad answered.

"I don't blame you," said the forester, "in fact I'm going to follow in your footsteps."

"Don't be a fool, Sandy," Dad sounded cross. "This is a personal matter and nothing to do with you."

"And mine's a personal matter too," answered the forester. "I don't like this Mr. Ross."

Dad had a short conference with the sawmill foreman and the estate carpenter about some window-frames that would be needed for the cottages on the new farm, which was apparently more or less bought, and he had to work very hard to keep the conversation brisk and to the point. It was obvious that they both wanted to say that they were sorry about the news and that Dad was trying to prevent them. We left abruptly and drove deep into the forest. We spent a long time there, bumping along tracks between plantations. Occasionally Dad pointed and said "Douglas firs," or "Norwegian spruce" but mostly he just looked grim. It was very quiet among the taller conifers, but when we came to the larch plantations and the mixed woods of beech and ash and oak there were birds singing as though it were spring. Dad stopped the Land Rover on a heath planted with tiny conifers and knee-high beeches and looked down on the patchwork of land below. We could see Nutsford and Charnworth, both the house and the village, and the down and the ranges of hills beyond. Farms, woods and fertile fields and the flood water all spread before us in the pale wintry sun.

Dad sighed. "It's a lovely place," he said, "but it's not

the only one," and then he drove off briskly and took the
lane for Castle Farm. Not much work was being done
there either. Two tractors stood in the yard with their
engines running and a group of men had gathered in the
building where the pig meal is ground. Dad sent me to
look at the pigs while he talked to the men.

At Cross Farm, where we went next, they told us that
Mr. Smithson had called in looking for Dad, and he'd
left word he was going to Wood End. When we were
back in the Land Rover, Dad gave me a conspiratorial
look. "We'll go to New Farm," he said, "I don't feel up
to facing him yet. Keep your eyes open for a brand new
Land Rover; he's stopped bumping that Bentley round
the lanes at last."

New Farm is high and windswept with huge fields,
mostly arable, and a small herd of Friesian cows. Mr.
Smithson had been there, we heard, looking for Mr.
Conway.

Dad said, "He's hit the heelway," and laughed and
when we'd inspected a tractor that someone had run
into a wall, and a leaking barn, we drove briskly down
hill, back to the shelter of the valley and then up again to
Ashmoor. The sheep are kept at Ashmoor and we visited
the breeding ewes; the Dorset horned with their
November lambs already penned out on the kale, and
the flock of Barset Down ewes who would lamb in the
early spring.

Everyone at Ashmoor was gloomy. They shook their
heads and said that they had known it would come to this
and that they were going to look round and see what else
they could find. Dad was bracing. He said that his
reasons for going were personal and that it was ridiculous for anyone else to leave without giving his

successor a trial. He even went so far as to tell the head shepherd that he thought Mr. Smithson would make a very good employer once he got the hang of country ways. We were back in the yard and Dad was arguing with one of the younger men, a tractor driver called Harry, who was threatening to join the Army because he was fed up with all the changes, when a new Land Rover swept in. "Ware Smithson," I said. Harry disappeared into the nearest barn as the F.W. approached. He was wearing a brand new riding macintosh and gleaming gumboots. "Good morning, Conway," he said, "I've been looking for you. Good morning, Douglas."

We answered unenthusiastically. Dad looked at me. "You'd better go and wait in the Land Rover," he said. I don't know whether he thought the Land Rover was soundproof because it wasn't. I felt that probably I oughtn't to listen, but short of blocking my ears and making a humming noise there was nothing much I could do; so I sat and bit my nails and listened to every word.

"I've been to see Martin," the F.W. began, "and I gather you have too. It seems to have been through a – a misunderstanding" – he was choosing his words carefully – "that the heifers were turned out on the meads. I know Ross upset Martin on Christmas Eve and it seems there was a rumour that you were leaving, but the real cause of the trouble was this cow, Carmen. I can't imagine why you let me send the matriarch of the herd to market."

Dad looked surprised; he hadn't expected this line of attack. "Well, if we're running the place on a commercial basis we can't keep old cows," he answered.

"Oh yes we can," the F.W. told him. "Our budget's not as tight as that. But I can't be expected to know which old cows are dear to the head herdsman and which can go for beef as a matter of course. And, as I see it, it's the Land Agent's job to tell me. I ought to have been given the full facts when this business about Carmen first came up."

"I couldn't say any more than I did," Dad objected. "Not without giving Ross the chance to go round telling everyone that I was a sentimental old fool."

"There are worse things to be called," said the F.W. calmly. "Now, about yesterday," he went on. "I'm sorry it happened; we'd all had a very nasty fright and you didn't altogether appreciate the facts. In the light of all this would you like to reconsider your resignation?"

I could have cheered. Go on, Dad, I thought, say yes. You know jolly well you don't want to go.

But Dad was standing there looking dismal and doubtful.

"You know that half the men on the estate are threatening to leave if you go?" said the F.W.

"Is that why you're asking me to stay?" asked Dad quickly.

"No, but I thought it might influence you."

"They won't go, they'll threaten, but their wives will talk them out of it."

"Martin's a widower, I believe," remarked the F.W. evenly.

Oh go *on*, Dad, I thought desperately. Why don't you say you'll stay?

But he continued to dither and at last the F.W. asked, "What is the difficulty?"

"Ross," Dad answered, "I quite appreciate that—"

The F.W. interrupted him. "I told Ross on Christmas Eve we wouldn't need him any more," he said.

Dad cheered up at once. "Oh well, in that case, of course I'll stay."

"Good," said the F.W. briskly. "Now I want a word with Douglas." He marched towards the Land Rover and I climbed out wondering what exactly Nick had told him. I found the direct gaze from behind the thick-lensed spectacles very intimidating.

"I understand that you have in your possession a certain cow," he said.

TWENTY

I looked at Dad. "We bought Carmen," I told him. "We didn't want her to go as dogs' meat so we took some money out of our post office accounts and went to Charlbury and bought her. We've been keeping her at the Firs."

"*You* bought Carmen?" exclaimed Dad explosively.

"Unfortunately," said the F.W., "I didn't know anything about it until last night when Nicholas told me, otherwise we might have sorted things out earlier. Still – there it is. Arrange to buy her back for me, Conway, will you? I've reason to suppose that the vendors will accept thirty pounds. And I'd like her delivered as soon as possible; I've already told Martin where she is, and when I left Home Farm he was bedding down her stall."

"I thought you said he was leaving," objected Dad.

"He was," a ghost of a smile hovered over the inscrutable features, "until I assured him that I would persuade you to stay." The F.W. made for his Land Rover and Dad and I stood and looked at each other.

"Well—" said Dad, and then as the F.W. drove out of the yard, he added, "Oh come on, let's go home. Fiona will be mad with joy."

I couldn't be mad with joy because there was still Shamrock to be revealed. It's now or never, I thought, and as soon as Dad had navigated the perilous turn into the road, I said, "I'm afraid we bought a horse as well as Carmen. She's at the Firs too."

"For heaven's sake, Douglas!" exclaimed Dad, and "I suppose in a minute you'll tell me you've got a flock of sheep up there too."

"No, only Carmen and Shamrock," I answered.

"And you bought the horse the day you went to Charlbury? The day you spent chasing Chieftain round?" He was looking at me suspiciously. I decided to tell him the whole story and when I'd finished, he said, "Well, you are a lot," and that was all he said because we had reached Nutsford. He drove dashingly up the front door hooting the horn gaily. "You go and tell the children," he said, jumping out and diving into the house, and as I ran towards the Old Kitchen I heard him shouting, "Fiona."

The atmosphere in the Old Kitchen was of the deepest gloom and it was wonderful to be able to shatter it by shouting "We're not going after all. The F.W.'s persuaded Dad to stay and he's going to buy Carmen back."

Andrew and Rory went mad; they gave war whoops and took wild leaps on to the furniture and finished up by standing on their heads. The girls were more restrained, they wanted to know how and why. I explained. "The F.W. was decent," I finished, "and he seems to have discovered how to manage Dad. Oh, and I confessed about Shamrock."

"We've had an awful morning," Cathy told me, "Nick came round but he only saw Penny and Rory and they wouldn't speak to him."

"Why should we?" asked Penny fiercely, "after all the lies he told us?"

"Oh lord! Well, let's forget him for a moment," I said. "We haven't got to leave Nutsford, that's the main thing, and we haven't any secret animals. And if we deliver Carmen directly after lunch we'll never have to milk her again, thank *goodness*."

Then Mum's voice began to call for layers and we avalanched to the kitchen. "We're going to have lunch early," she explained, "so that you can fetch these animals from the Firs directly afterwards. You are an awful lot, really. I'm sure other people's children don't do things like that."

"Badly brought up and who's to blame?" I answered, trying to juggle with the table mats.

As we ate turkey risotto the telephone rang and Mum said, "Oh I expect that's Monica, she was going to ring; I'll go," and hurried to the sitting-room. A few moments later she reappeared looking rather startled. "John," she said, "it's Mrs. Smithson. They want us to go in to drinks at six this evening, and take all the children."

"Oh damn the man," said Dad, "he might give me time to recover; I still feel flattened from this morning."

"What shall I say?" asked Mum.

"Yes, of course," Dad answered. "We can't refuse."

When Mum came back again she told us that Mrs. F.W. had been nice. "She said not to dress up as their Christmas visitors have gone and it'll be only them. And she's determined to have all you children."

Andrew and Rory were looking rather horrified at the ordeal and Penny was red in the face. "I don't want to go," she said, "I'm not going to speak to Nick."

"Oh Penny," said Mum reproachfully.

Dad spoke briskly, "Well, if the relations have gone, the boy will have gone too, so you won't have to speak to him." And we all thought that probably Dad was right. "I expect he came to say good-bye this morning," observed Cathy sadly. And it seemed sad to me too, that our friendship with Nick should end in such a mess, but I was anxious to forget his puzzling Jekyll and Hyde behaviour and to enjoy our good fortune. I got up and began to clear away the plates. After lunch Cathy and Rory set off for the Firs on the ponies and Dad said that he would run the rest of us up in the Land Rover. All the way there Penny told him how awful Shamrock looked and how he'd feel sick when he saw her. I did wish Penny would stop fussing over details, I wanted peace in which to gloat over Charnworth.

Dad didn't come into the Firs, he said he'd go home and join the reception committee. Penny, Andrew and I sat on the gate and waited impatiently for Cathy and Rory. Then, when they arrived we turned the ponies loose, gave them masses of hay and caught Shamrock and Carmen. We told Carmen that she was going back to her electric milking machine and her huge meals and when she found herself on the road and going towards Charnworth she began to hurry. Shamrock was feeling better, she even managed to shy. She shied at a dog, at two peculiar stones, four garden gates and a pile of grit and she also made a film-starish fuss about stepping into thin sheets of flood water which flowed across the road on either side of the bridge. But when she pranced and dithered she looked quite a decent sort of horse, so we all felt pleased and even Penny became less gloomy about what Dad was going to say. The parents were waiting on the doorstep when we reached home, and Dad rushed to inspect Carmen. He announced that she looked well and that we had not given her mastitis or any other evil and then he turned his attention to Shamrock, whom Mum was already stuffing with sugar. Dad looked at her for a bit, while we all waited expectantly and then opened her mouth and began to laugh. "Did you know you'd bought a three-year-old?" he asked.

"The man said she was seven," Penny told him.

"I never looked at her teeth," I admitted remembering that I'd been too angry.

"I expect she's a racing stable cast-out, too slow or too small or something." Dad said. "Probably someone bought her fairly cheap and didn't realise she was going to need a lot of looking after. She may grow into quite a nice little horse."

"I think she's a sweetie," observed Mum. "But are they ever going to manage her when she's fit?"

"They'll have to learn to," answered Dad, "they can't go on riding Merlin for ever."

We put Shamrock in a loose box with masses to eat and then we set off for Home Farm leading Carmen. Or rather she led us. She trotted most of the way, a purposeful expression on her face, and when she reached Home Farm she towed Cathy across the yard to the cow byre and into her rightful stall. We called for Mr. Martin and he came limping across the yard with a huge bucket full of superior cakes and cubes and behind him came George White with an armful of choice hay.

"Well, I never thought we'd see old Carmen back, never," said Bill Martin as he watched her gobbling greedily. "And you 'ad me on proper," said George

White turning to us, "told me you were Christmas shopping and all the time you were waiting to buy 'er. And then to think she's been up at the Firs all this time."

"Never thought to set eyes on her again," said Bill Martin. We began to edge our way out. George saw us to the gate. "Poor old Bill," he said, "'e's 'ad a time lately. Still, he'll be all right now 'e's got Carmen back and things are settling down. Not that you can count on these Londoners, 'ere today and gone tomorrow, that's what I say."

We went home and collapsed in exhausted attitudes all over the Old Kitchen and we stayed there until Mum appeared and began to fuss about what we were going to wear. We pointed out that Mrs. F.W. had said not to dress up, but Mum retorted that the F.W. was always dressed up by our standards and made us clean our shoes. After tea she put on a wool frock which she said was "suitable" and Dad, who'd been out spreading the good news round the farms, changed into a tweed suit. Andrew and I wore grey flannel trousers, shirts, Christmas ties and hacking jackets, Rory jeans and his best pullover and the girls tartan skirts, pullovers and their new bracelets. Mum inspected us and announced that all our hair needed cutting, but that at least we looked clean.

Then filled with fear and trepidation, or at least I was, we embarked in the Land Rover. Mum made Dad drive about a mile an hour up the back drive because she'd discovered that it was only four and a half minutes past six and she said that London people thought it un-sophisticated to arrive for drinks on time.

An Italian manservant showed us into the oak-panelled hall which everyone who lives at Charnworth seems to use as their everyday sitting-room. It was much warmer and rather less gloomy than I remembered it so I supposed that changes had taken place inside the house too. The F.W. hurried to meet us – he was wearing cavalry twill trousers and a hacking jacket and he introduced us all to Mrs. F.W., who hadn't dressed up at all but was wearing a pair of very dashingly tapered slacks and a huge pullover. The F.W. seemed to know all our names which was a little disconcerting; I couldn't help wondering what else he knew. Mrs. F.W., who was very vivacious, began a conversation with both parents at once while the F.W. poured drinks. The others were all talking to a small black poodle and a Siamese cat who sat side by side on the hearthrug, but Dad made a face at me which meant "make yourself useful", so I had to go and offer to hand round. When he'd poured out for the grown-ups the F.W. asked what we drank and we said "Anything", so he gave Cathy and me each about half a glass of sherry and the others orange squash. Then he said "Catherine and Douglas, I want to talk to you," and manœuvred us into a quiet corner of the room. Cathy and I looked at each other and sipped our sherry nervously. "It's about Nicholas," explained the F.W. "He's refused to appear this evening because he says that none of you ever want to speak to him again. He's very upset. I think he values your friendship greatly – more perhaps than you realise."

I said, "It's only Penny who's not speaking."

"I know," the F.W. went on, "but the point is that he doesn't blame any of you for being angry, he says that he's made a mess of things and I thought that perhaps, since he's told me a good many of your secrets, I might straighten things out by telling you his."

The F.W. took a sip of his sherry and fixed me with an unfathomable glare.

"Nicholas's parents are divorced," he went on, "and lately they've both re-married and, for reasons I won't go into, neither pair want him. As we haven't any children we're delighted to have him, but his parents' desertion has been, well, a shattering blow, and he hasn't accepted it yet; he spends a lot of his time inventing new parents, who are absent for exciting and unavoidable reasons. Of course their name is never Smithson. I think that was what he was doing when he met you."

We nodded. Looking from one to the other of us the F.W. went on, "And then, I gather, you made it rather difficult for him to admit his identity."

I suppose we looked as embarrassed as we felt because he added, "Well, never mind about that, and on the whole it was a good thing. I'm sure we would all have gone on being suspicious of each other for very much longer if Nicholas hadn't been in the position to – er – spill the beans."

Gradually I saw and understood it all. The things which had puzzled me about Nick fell one by one into place. Of course he'd run from the fire, he'd seen his uncle coming and known that we would learn who he really was. No wonder he hadn't wanted to meet our parents. And every word we'd uttered had made it more and more difficult for him to explain.

Cathy said, "Poor Nick," and the F.W. looked at me. "How do you feel about it, Douglas?" he asked. "Oh, 'poor Nick' too," I answered. "But I don't suppose he wants to be pitied. You'd better tell him that we quite understand and that he wasn't the only idiot," I felt

myself growing red in the face, "that we've been pretty
dumb too."

"I think I'll see if I can get him to come down," said
the F.W. and left the room. I suddenly felt rather sorry
for him. He had spent the day having man-to-man talks
with the Conways and now he'd got to have another
with Nick.

Cathy muttered something about telling Penny. I
looked at the pictures without really seeing them, my
mind was still on Nick.

Then the door opened and the F.W. ushered him in.
He wore a grey suit, a white shirt and a rather flashy tie.
I said, "Hi, Nick," in false and hearty tones and Nick
sort of drooped. The F.W. said he'd get Nick some
sherry and would I like some more, but being on my best
behaviour I answered that I'd better not.

With the F.W. out of the way things were a bit easier.
"Isn't it splendid," I said, "that all this fuss and muddle is
over and now we can settle down to enjoy the rest of the
holidays? Carmen's back at Home Farm," I went on,
"but I expect the – I mean your uncle told you that."

"He knows you call him the F.W.," said Nick in a
toneless voice. "I told him; he doesn't mind." For a
moment I felt like turning on Nick and telling him he
was a creep; I think it was what he expected me to do,
but then I remembered that he knew we'd been told
about his parents and that he must be feeling pretty
naked too, and in a way that hurt much more. So I said,
"All right, you've told the F.W. everything; but he
doesn't mind and we don't care now let's forget it."
Then mercifully the F.W. brought Nick's sherry and
with him came Cathy and Penny. Cathy said, "I hear
you're going to have a horse, Nick." "Are you?" I

asked, "that's great." I began to calculate. "Five of us will be able ride at once."

"I won't have a horse-box or a coat with a velvet collar or ride at The Horse of the Year Show," said Nick, looking a bit more cheerful.

We laughed when we remembered that conversation. "You should have shut us up," Cathy told him.

"I tried to sometimes," he answered. He had, and I realised that now, remembering with embarrassment several conversations.

Nick looked at Penny, who seemed to be lurking behind Cathy and said, "I've spoken to Uncle Dan about having a cross-country course in Castle Woods; he said he thought it would be all right, but he'd have to ask your father." The fact of the F.W. being someone's Uncle Dan made him seem more human and the thought of him asking Dad for permission for us to have a cross-country course in Castle Woods seemed positively funny. Even Penny cheered up and they all began to talk at once. I looked round the room. Mrs. F.W. was still talking to both the parents and the F.W., Andrew and Rory were all gathered round the drinks cabinet. As far as I could make out Andrew and Rory were trying all the various soft drinks in turn. Rory seemed to be in command and the F.W. stood, obediently opening little bottle after little bottle. I went across to investigate. Andrew handed his glass to me. "Try some bitter lemon, Douglas," he said, "it's pretty good."

"Try some ginger ale," said Rory, forcing another glass on me, "it's the most disgusting awful lousy drink I ever tasted."

"Rory!" objected Andrew in shocked tones.

"Well, I only meant compared with the others,"

Rory explained. He picked up another bottle. "Tonic water" he read out. "What's that like?"

"Dull," answered the F.W. and waited patiently with the bottle opened poised.

"May as well try it," decided Rory. At any minute, I thought, he'll address the F.W. as "Mate" but perhaps, I consoled myself, as he already knows so much about us it won't matter. We had somehow skipped the "best behaviour" stage in our relationship. We'd all gone through so much it was as though we'd known each other for years; we were almost old friends.

Then Nick came over. "Happy New Year, Douglas," he said, raising his glass.

"You're too early, still three days to go," I objected, but Mrs. F.W. had taken up the cry and the F.W. hurried to refill the empty glasses.

"Happy New Year," we wished each other all smiling. Suddenly I knew that the hideous and traumatic events which had ruined the beginning of the holidays were truly over and a very different sort of year was about to begin.